SEVEN TALES

For Chandra!

Seven Tales

G.C. McRae

MacDonald Warne Media

Seven Tales, by G.C.McRae
Published by MacDonald Warne Media

Cover and Interior Design by Dianna Little
Ornaments by Margaret Rose

ISBN: 978-0-9939183-4-6

Fiction/Fairy Tales

Seven Tales is produced only in eco-friendly POD and eBook editions.

Visit us at: www.gcmcrae.com

Contents

The Seven Sisters

The Seven Sisters

There was once a king who treated his people very badly. Even though they were starving, he spent all their tax money on cheese and crowns and fancy socks. After a while, the people grew tired of this king. So they took him out to a big tree one day and strung him up by his small toes.

Now, this king had a timid brother. He had his own kingdom and he was so afraid of being strung up by his small toes that he never acted without consulting his ministers and advisors. For if anything went wrong, he could blame it on them and they would be strung up instead.

The king wore the same clothes every day. Someone once said he looked nice in them, and it made him worry that they didn't like any of his other clothes. And he always ate the same thing for his dinner every night. If he didn't, the people might say he was spending too much of their tax money on extravagances.

The king had not always been so timid, especially years before when his queen was alive. She had been the sort of person who didn't care what anyone thought or did, as long as it had some sense to it. But she had died giving birth to their last child, their seventh daughter. Since then the king had withdrawn into himself, always afraid bad things were going to happen. And try as he might, he could deny his daughters nothing, for he'd much rather have them spoiled than angry with him.

A few years passed, and the king's people pressured him to remarry, for everyone wants their country to have both a king and a queen. So the king, not wanting to make a mistake and fall in love with the wrong person, gave the task of finding a new queen over to his ministers and advisors. They decided that the best choice was the spinster daughter of a certain lord of a distant region. But before she would marry the king and become queen of his land, she wanted to know what she was getting into. So she sent the king several letters asking what it was like there.

Does your castle have many drafty rooms? I have a tendency to sneeze in a drafty room.

The king wrote back that no, he did not have any drafty rooms at all, but he called in his ministers and had them check all of the rooms to make sure that this was true.

Does the courtyard have brightly coloured flags around it? I love to wake in the morning and see bright flags fluttering in the breeze.

The king called in his ministers and ordered a hundred brightly coloured flags made, to be hung all around the courtyard. *Yes,* he wrote back to the future queen, *we have many brightly coloured flags around our courtyard.*

Well, she wrote back, *that is good. I like you more and more. But do you have a garden where I can walk among the flowers in the evening?*

The king called in his ministers and had them begin construction of a beautiful flower garden. *Oh, yes,* he wrote back, *we have a wonderful garden where you can walk in the evenings.*

But then the king received a letter from her that upset him very much. *Do you have,* asked the future queen, *any children? One child is sometimes a comfort, but I cannot stand to have many children running around all the time. Especially not young ones.*

When the king got this letter he called a big meeting with all his ministers and advisors and asked them what he should do. For he really did want to have this woman for his wife, and didn't want to displease her. The ministers and advisors all hummed and hawed for a long while, some pulling on their beards, some scratching their heads.

Then one of them spoke up: "Your Majesty, you should tell our future queen that you do have a child, but that she is not too young. Do not say you have seven daughters, but merely say that, yes, you do have a daughter, which is true."

"But she will discover them all eventually, won't she?" asked the king.

"Not if you follow my advice," said the minister. "Your daughters all have a striking resemblance to each other, except for their ages. They all have long brown hair, they all have blue, blue eyes, and they are all very slender. Tell the queen you have one daughter and let the youngest six live in a far corner of the castle where the queen will never go. We will all tell her it is dangerous to go there, or that it is dusty, or it is dark. When the eldest grows up and goes off to be married, let the next oldest take her place, and the queen will never know."

The king sat with his mouth open, looking to see what all the other ministers and advisors thought. When they all began smiling and nodding to each other, the king said, "Brilliant idea! We shall do it." So a letter was written, the lady was satisfied, and soon the king found himself with a new wife and queen and happier subjects than he had known in a long time.

The eldest daughter was given her own room at the front of the castle, with closets full of fancy dresses. She was allowed to go to all the balls and concerts and dances and eat in the main hall with the grown-ups.

The younger girls, being promised the same when they were older, were just as content as their eldest sister. They were given a huge room at the far end of the castle. Being young and away from the public eye, they could wear their play clothes from morning to night. And they never had to comb their hair or wash their faces because no one would see them anyway.

The king would visit them in the evenings, when the queen was taking her walk among the flowers in the garden. He would bring them toys and trinkets and sweets because he felt guilty over banishing his dear, lovely girls. He even tended to play with them more often than he would have otherwise.

The queen was quite happy in her new home. She was even happier when she discovered how timid the king was. For the king never argued with her and always let her have her way. She wanted a servant to do her hair in braids and another one to paint her face and fingernails and he hired both new servants for her. She wanted a pond with swans for the garden and he had a huge pond dug and swans caught and brought there. She even wanted a mirror put on every wall of every room of the castle so she would always know how beautiful she looked, and though the king rolled his eyes at this, he eventually had the mirrors installed despite the enormous cost of them all.

Well, the time came when the king's eldest daughter fell in love with a prince at one of the fancy dress balls. She wanted to marry him and move away to his castle. The king had secretly dreaded this moment, knowing it would be the real test of his ministers' grand plan to keep the queen content. But his ministers and advisors told the king not to worry, that they would take care of everything.

So, the eldest daughter went off with her prince and married him without the queen's knowledge. The next day, the second oldest daughter was brought from the far room and put into her sister's clothes and shoes and given the room at the front of the castle.

For a few days the queen and the new daughter chanced not to meet each other. But when they did, the queen looked sideways at the girl, sensing something was wrong, but not quite knowing what. "Are you all right, my dear?" she asked.

The girl had been coached by the ministers to tell the queen that she had been feeling ill lately, so she said, "I have a cold, and fear I have lost a little weight."

The queen kept studying her face and looking at her strangely. Then she said, "Perhaps you should see the court physician, my dear."

"Oh, I have already," said the girl, repeating what the ministers had told her to say. "He has given me the most excellent medicine."

"Indeed..." said the queen, and continued on her way. But she thought, *That girl doesn't look sick, she looks even healthier than she did the other day. How strange...* However, she had asked the king to order her a whole new closet full of ball gowns, and they were arriving today, so she thought little more of it.

Two years passed. The second eldest daughter was growing into a fine young woman and everyone in the castle was full of praise for her grace, her gentleness, and her beauty. The queen was a little jealous of her, but made sure, with her gowns and hairstyles and experience in courtly ways, that she remained the centre of attention at feasts and balls held in the castle.

But then this second eldest daughter secretly married and moved away. The third oldest girl was brought from the far room to take her place. The queen ran into her in the great hall on her first day as "only daughter," and thought something was definitely amiss.

"Are you all right, my dear?" the queen asked of this younger and more beautiful stepdaughter.

"I have a cold," said the girl, repeating the words the ministers had told her to say, "and fear I have lost a little weight."

And the queen said, "Perhaps you should see the court physician, my dear."

"Oh, I have already," answered the girl, "and he has given me the most wonderful medicine."

"Indeed..." said the queen. Just then she glimpsed herself in a mirror and saw that there were lines of age appearing on her face. She also saw how beautiful this little slip of a girl was and the comparison irked her.

So it went, year after year, the eldest princess carrying on the ruse for a time, then meeting a prince or young nobleman and secretly leaving to marry him, and the next oldest daughter taking her place. All this time the queen was getting older, and the princess appeared to remain not merely young, but more beautiful and graceful as each year passed.

With each turn of renewed youth and beauty in the girl, the queen had a turn of anger with her own advancing age. And she showed this anger in odder and odder ways. She fired the servants who did her hair and makeup and had two well-known experts brought from afar to replace them. They were very expensive, but when she broke out in spots from the powders they used, they had to be fired too.

The next year she had all her beloved mirrors covered. But that wasn't enough. A few months later she compelled the king to have every mirror, not just in the castle, but in the entire kingdom, destroyed. By the time the fifth daughter was married off and the sixth took her place, the queen was so jealous she had the king tell the girl she could only wear one particular, unbecoming dress so she wouldn't outshine the queen.

Then, the queen made the strangest of all her demands: she ordered the king to proclaim that no old woman should live or be seen within several miles of the castle, lest the queen be reminded of her advancing age. At this the king tried to put his foot down and refuse. But the queen kept at him so mercilessly, refusing to speak of anything else till she had her way, that eventually the king gave in and passed the law. He regretted his decision from that day forward, but not as much as the townspeople regretted wanting a new queen so badly, for now everyone's mother and grandmother had to live far away.

Then came the day when the far room was empty and the youngest girl took her sister's place in the fine room at the front of the castle and assumed the role of the king's only daughter. More than twelve years had passed since the queen had first come to the castle. Twelve years in which the lines on her face had deepened, the hair at her temples turned to grey. Though she was still beautiful for her age, it pained her more and more to know that everyone, right down to the lowest kitchen boy, could see how her beauty was fading into an inevitable autumn.

The one dress that the girls had been compelled to wear was now quite torn and shabby. But the girl who now wore it, the king's youngest daughter, was the fairest beauty of all the sisters. She made her first appearance in the great hall looking much like a fine piece of china that a maid had accidently left covered with an old dusting rag. Tatters on such youthful beauty ensured that all eyes in the great hall were upon her, admiring, pitying, questioning. At the sight of the king's youngest daughter on this evening, the queen went pale and felt as if every grey hair was made of ice and every line was a crack that would break her. She sat with her jaw clenched the entire evening. Or rather, for part of the evening, for midway through the meal she rose and without a word to anyone, she retired to her chambers.

Two days passed in which the queen refused to leave her room. On the evening of the third day she went for a walk in her beloved garden, only to find there had been a killing frost the night before and most of the leaves and flowers were wilted. In tears, she turned to go back to her chamber and saw her stepdaughter at the edge of the garden pond, feeding the swans.

The queen strode toward her, surprising the girl, who looked up with a start.

"Are you all right, my dear?" the queen asked with undisguised sarcasm. She could see plainly the radiance of youth in the girl's face.

"I—I—" the girl fumbled, trying, in her surprise, to remember the words she had been told to say.

"You have a cold," said the queen.

"Yes!" said the girl, forgetting to play her part.

"And you have lost a little weight," said the queen.

The girl suddenly understood the queen's intention and looked down at her hands, which were toying with a bit of bread she had brought for the swans.

"Perhaps you should see the court physician, my dear."

"Oh," said the girl, remembering her lines and the peril she would be in if the trick were discovered. "I...I have seen him already and he has given me some nice medicine."

"Indeed," said the queen. Grasping the girl's arm, she pulled her to her feet and said, "Why don't we go and see the court physician and he can tell us what is in this medicine."

The queen brought the girl into the castle and straight to the physician's room where she knocked loudly on the door.

The hour was getting late by then and the physician, who was a near-sighted little man, came to the door with a candle. "Yes? Oh!" he said, "It is you, Your Majesty." Then he saw the princess and the queen's grip on her arm, and immediately understood what was going on. He let out another little "Oh!" as the queen pulled the girl past him into the room.

"Your Majesty, how...how may I be of assistance?" The doctor knew he was in serious trouble, for it had been many years since the king's ministers had instructed him on what to say to the queen, should she inquire.

The queen seemed to tower over the little doctor. "I understand you have been treating my stepdaughter for a cold," she said, and then added, "for many years."

"Yes. Yes, I have, Your Majesty," said the little doctor.

"And what might this medicine be?" asked the queen. "This medicine that keeps a girl so young for so long?" The candle quivered in the doctor's hand as he searched for an answer. But the queen stepped even closer to add, "And why have you kept it from your queen all this time?"

The doctor looked from the queen to the girl, who was making a face that said, *My, are you ever in trouble,* and stammered, "You...you have been in excellent health all these years, Your Majesty. I had no reason to prescribe you my remedy."

The queen took a deep breath, as if drawing in her fury, making her seem even taller to the doctor. "I expect a large bottle of it on my table in the morning," she said. "A very large bottle." And she flung the girl's arm from her and stormed from the room.

The girl, who had been sure for a moment that the queen had discovered their secret, was so relieved by this strange turn of events that she couldn't help but giggle when the queen was gone. For to her, it was very much a game at this point. Having lived most of her life at the far end of the castle, she had no particular attachment to this woman, this wife of her father's.

But the poor doctor was stricken with terror at the thought of being burdened with someone else's twelve-year lie. How could he get out of it? How could he pretend to make a remedy for the queen that would supposedly restore her to youth? The greatest minds in history had puzzled over this and not one had found an answer. What was he to do?

The girl pulled gently on his shirtsleeve. "Don't worry," she said. "If she's so blind she can be fooled for twelve years, it'll take her another twelve to figure out that the medicine isn't working. Just whip her up something foul tasting and think no more about it."

The doctor gave her a sad, pained look and patted her hand. "You're right," he said. "At least it will buy me some time."

The following morning the queen awoke, sat straight up in bed, and looked at her night table. There stood a bottle as big and as round as pumpkin, full to its cork with bluish liquid. The queen's eyes lit up. She called for a maid and a spoon and had the maid give her three big doses of the remedy. It tasted so foul it brought tears to her eyes and she coughed and sniffled for the next half-hour. But she fully believed that the potion would restore her to youth, and called for a mirror to see what effect the dosing had on her.

"I'm sorry, My Lady," said the maid, "but you had all the mirrors in the kingdom destroyed. It will take some time to fetch one from afar."

"How do I look?" demanded the queen. "Do I look younger? More beautiful? Less wrinkly? Tell me, quick!"

The maid studied the queen's face for some time and at last declared, "Yes, I...I do believe there is some change."

The queen fell back on the bed with a smile and a sigh. "Call me when you find a mirror," she said, and rubbed her cheeks to make the remedy work faster.

Three days passed before one of the royal messengers at last found a mirror and rushed it to the castle for the queen. She was feeling extraordinarily well during those three days, she told everyone. She could even be seen out in the garden actually helping the gardeners, raking up the autumn leaves and pruning the hedges before winter. “I am a new woman,” she said. “Here, feel my face, isn’t it soft? Doesn’t it make you think of a child’s skin? Oh, I feel so new and alive!”

When the queen heard that the mirror had arrived, she rushed into the castle and nearly knocked over the waiting messenger. “Let me see the change, let me see!” Grabbing the mirror from his hands, she looked at her face and saw the same crow’s-feet beside her eyes, saw the same grey complexion, the same withering skin and yellowing teeth.

Then she looked at the people around her—the maid, the gardeners coming in, and the messenger—and said, “You’re all laughing. You’re all making a fool of me. There is no magic remedy, is there? You’re all laughing and thinking I’m a fool!” And she threw the mirror across the hall where it smashed on the stone floor, and stormed from the room, her face a picture of mad hopelessness.

When the princess heard all this she covered her mouth with her hand, knowing she shouldn’t laugh but unable to help it. “It serves her right,” she declared. “She put my sisters and I and all the kingdom through a great deal of trouble for nothing, for her own vanity. I suppose it is only right she suffer a little now.”

But that night, the girl's own maidservant woke her some hours before the sun was up. "What is it?" she asked, and for some time all she heard were the sobs of her maid in the dark. "Here, light a candle, will you? What's wrong?"

The maid lit a candle from an ember still glowing in the fireplace, then came and sat on the girl's bed and wiped her eyes. "Our good doctor has been killed," she said at last. "His body was found in the great hall. The queen has killed him and wants everyone to know it. She defies the king to punish her."

Now the young princess was not laughing. She had liked the little doctor very much. He had tended her and her sisters, curing their ills their entire lives. Then she remembered that she was the one who had gotten the doctor into trouble to begin with. She was the one who had laughingly suggested he make the foul-tasting potion for the queen. Though it was all her fault, the doctor, the innocent doctor, was the one who had died for her silly idea.

She rose, dressed quickly, and went to see her father, who was leaning on a windowsill in the great hall, staring blankly out into dark nothing. Servants were carrying the body of the doctor from the room. The huge round bottle the doctor had prepared for the queen lay smashed against a wall.

"Father, what are we going to do about this? She can't kill whoever she pleases to have her way."

The king sat slowly on the windowsill and looked up at her for a long time, his pleading eyes telling the girl everything. "I am a failure," he said. "This murder of the doctor is nothing next to the shame I face for having let it happen. I am no more than a pathetic servant to the queen. Everything she asked for, I gave her. Now the people hate me for spending their tax money on the queen's every whim. They hate me for banishing the mirrors and all the old women. Now you, too, are against me. I cannot bear it." With a weak wave of his hand, he told the girl to leave him alone in his helpless grief.

So she left, determined not to be caught in this string of foolishness and prepared to do whatever was necessary to set everything to rights. She called her most trusted servant and asked her to send messengers to summon her six sisters, but to tell them to come by night and not be seen. They would meet in their old playroom before the new moon. And so it was done.

For the next two weeks the girl kept to her room to avoid the queen, saying she was ill. She was hoping, in her young mind, that without a doctor to treat her illness, it might keep people's attention on the queen's horrible crime. When all the sisters had arrived, glad to be together for any reason, even an unpleasant one, the seven met and talked about what must be done. And a plan was formed.

The following morning, the youngest girl showed herself about the castle and toward noon met the hated queen in the garden. "You should not have been so hasty with the remedy," the girl said. The queen, seeming more miserable than ever, looked askance at her, not knowing what she meant. "The potion takes seven days to take effect. It does not come on gradually, but on the evening of the seventh day it happens all at once. Now you have thrown away the potion and the only man who knew how to make it is dead."

"Ha!" said the queen. "Such lies from so young a mouth. How can I know there is any truth to what you say?"

"You will see," said the girl. "For with the doctor dead I have run out of the remedy myself. As long as you and I took that potion, we held back the bowstring of age. But in quitting the potion, we have let the arrow fly. You will see how far."

The next morning the girl who chanced to meet the queen in the great hall, dressed just as the youngest princess had been in the garden the day before, was not the same sister, but the next oldest one. The queen thought little of this apparently aging girl. But by the fourth day, with the fourth oldest sister playing the part of the only daughter, the queen was convinced, and took to her bedroom in agonies of remorse.

The girls made a point of being seen by the queen at least once a day, either coming into the room unexpectedly or appearing before the queen's window in the garden. The queen was now in mortal horror over killing the only man who could have made and kept her young and beautiful. As each day passed, what remained of the queen's beauty faded and fell from her completely. By week's end, her unkempt hair was white as chalk, her cheeks sunken and withered.

On the evening of the seventh day, she expected the rapidly aging girl to visit her again and every knock at the door made her sit up in terror. But no one came. No one came to see her for three days after, and the queen kept to her room with the curtains drawn, terrified of catching sight of the princess's tattered dress in the garden outside.

Then one night came a faint knock at the queen's bedroom door. She was not expecting anyone but knew immediately who it was. The queen stayed in her bed, the covers drawn up to her chin. The door opened and into the room came a very, very old woman wearing the tattered dress the princesses had worn for so many years. Her back was bent so that her head almost touched the top of her gnarled cane. Her pure white hair hung in shreds over the shoulders of the dress. As she approached the bed she pointed a grim finger at the queen and said, "See what you have done! See what you could have prevented!" But by that time the queen had died of fright, sitting up in bed, the covers still held up to her chin.

The seven sisters had gone out and brought all the old women back to the town outside the castle. They asked one old soul to play the part of the girl, and offered to pay her for her trouble. But the old woman said no, she wanted nothing in payment for ridding the land of this wicked queen. It was a pleasure to help the girls in their hour of need and a wonderful thing to be able to return home to her family. No, no, she wanted no money for her trouble. But, she asked before she hobbled out, was there even a single drop of that doctor's remedy left?

The Boy Smith

and the Giant of the North

The Boy Smith and the Giant of the North

There was once a boy who was very unhappy working in his father's blacksmith shop. All day he had to burn big heaps of wood to make charcoal for the forge. He hated singeing his fingers. He hated getting smoke in his eyes. But most of all, he hated doing the same boring thing, day after day.

"Why do I have to make charcoal all the time?" he complained. Nothing his father did ever seemed to be boring. He was always working the hot iron, twisting, bending and hammering it into wonderful things. And to the boy's eyes, the most wonderful of all were the swords and battle-axes up on the wall of the shop. That was what he wanted to make.

"My boy," said his father, "I'm not so young anymore and making the charcoal hurts my lungs. Since your mother died, it's just the two of us here. I know charcoal-making is boring, but it has to be done. When you're older you can become my apprentice, and I'll show you how to make all the wonderful things. But you have to work hard and prove yourself."

Eager to leave all the burning and the smoke behind, the boy worked very hard. He ignored his sore fingers and watering eyes, knowing that an apprenticeship would take him away from making charcoal. Eventually his father came to him and said, "You have done so well, I am going to make you my apprentice. I'll be glad to have you hammer the hot iron, as I'm getting old and every day, my arms are aching."

The boy was glad for a change. He got to heat up the iron and hammer it till the sparks flew. When he was done he'd dip it into a barrel of water and it would hiss as it cooled off. He made spoons and knives for the kitchen and scythes and plow blades for the farm. But after a few years he grew tired of hammering. Hot iron dripped off and burned his toes. And though he grew strong, his arms were painfully sore at the end of every day. "I hate this!" he said. "I'm so sick of hammering. When can I do something else?"

His father answered, "You can do something else only when you're skilled enough. Then I'll make you a journeyman blacksmith. But you'll have to work hard for that."

So the boy eyed the beautiful swords and battle-axes up on the wall and worked harder than ever. Finally, the day came when his father decided it was time for a change. "You are so skilled now, I'm happy to make you a journeyman. My old back hurts from standing all day, so I need the help. You can be in charge of finishing and polishing everything we make."

"Well, that's wonderful," said the boy. "I'm so sick of making spoons and plow blades. Can I make swords and battle-axes now?"

His father laughed. "No, we don't make those anymore. The wars have been over for many years. And in peace-time, you can't till a field with a battle-axe."

The boy could not believe his ears. "Father, I will surely die if I have to spend one more minute making pot handles." He threw down his apron and said, "I quit!"

As he was packing up his bags, his father came to him. "I have spent all these years teaching you for nothing! What am I to do in my old age?"

Though the boy was feeling very bitter, he loved his father. "I am happy to take care of you in your old age," he said, "but not like this. I promise I will return. And my life and your old age will be far better than if I stayed."

So off the boy went, sad to leave his father, but determined to do any job but this, so he'd never be bored again. He spent many weeks wandering the countryside. He told no one he was a smith, wanting to put his early years behind him and learn something new. So he shovelled manure for farmers and kept out of the rain in their barns. He picked apples for an old woman so he could have something to eat and slept in the coop with her chickens.

Whenever he went to the great house of a lord or other nobleman, he asked about serving there and always received the same answer: "Who are you and where is your family? Why don't you have a trade? You're no good without one." So the boy thought he would travel to the heart of the kingdom and try his luck at the royal court.

On his way there, he chanced to meet an errant knight, the eldest son of a famous lord from a far country. The knight wanted nothing to do with him at first. But when the boy began making himself useful around the knight's camp, he relented and let him stay and share his meal. As it turned out, the knight was on his way to court too, though for another reason altogether.

It seemed the princess of the realm wanted to marry, but as soon as this was announced, the castle was visited by every fool, scallywag and potlick in the kingdom. The princess didn't mind. She liked all the attention. But it drove the king and queen mad to have young men crowding the great hall of their castle, eating their food and lounging on every chair and stair. What was worse, their daughter paraded around grinning and batting her eyes, as if having hundreds of admirers were somehow normal for a young lady.

Though the king was known to be very wise, he could also be quite heavy-handed. So the queen usually handled matters concerning the princess. The queen began by having a talk with her daughter about her behaviour, advising her on how she should dress and what she should say. The princess ignored everything her mother told her and continued flouncing around.

Next, the queen stood at the door, inspecting the suitors one at a time. She ordered those who smelled bad to have a bath. Those with poor manners, she scolded on the spot. And those with no teeth, she simply sent away. Needless to say, the princess was horrified by this, and loudly said so.

After many arguments with her daughter, the queen thought she had a solution. To keep the number of suitors reasonable and keep the riff-raff out, she decreed that only knights and noblemen could apply to be suitors for the princess's hand.

Still, the castle was overrun by every duke and count and their idiot son for a thousand miles around. The queen ended up fighting with her daughter so constantly, she finally went to the king and said, "She's your daughter, too. It's time for your heavy hand."

The king pondered the problem for some time. He needed to please his daughter and his queen and somehow end up with grandchildren who weren't idiots and didn't spend their days lolling around the great hall.

"So," the knight told the boy, "the king decided he would set four tasks for the suitors. Each task would be more difficult than the last, and impossible for anyone but a true hero to accomplish."

"What are these tasks?" asked the boy.

The knight looked down his nose at him and answered, "The first task is known to all. But the second, third and fourth tasks will only be revealed once the first one is completed."

"And what is the first task?"

"The first impossible task is to deliver into the king's hand a single ear of barley from the field of a giant who lives in the North."

"Well, that shouldn't be so difficult," said the boy.

"Aye, it shouldn't," said the knight, smoothing his perfectly trimmed moustaches. "Yet three dozen good men, all of them knights, princes, or noble lords, have tried and failed.

"The giant is said to be as tall as the sky and the sweat of his brow makes clouds over his barley field. Though his field stretches across a huge valley, he is ever watchful and tends and pampers every stalk as if it were his child." The knight puffed out his chest. "I shall be the first to succeed, and show the princess I am worthy of her hand."

Now this, thought the boy, was the sort of job he was looking for—a great adventure that was far from boring. So he got down on one knee and asked to be the knight's page, to serve him loyally, come what may. At first the knight said no, he had no need of a page. But the boy pleaded and promised and pestered the knight until finally he changed his mind.

So together, they travelled to the heart of the kingdom to try the king's impossible tasks.

When they arrived at the castle, the knight was greeted with every courtesy. He was introduced to the king and the queen and all their counsellors and he was given a fancy room with a broad view of the town and the countryside beyond. That evening at the royal table, as the boy served his noble master, he watched the knight being introduced to the princess.

The knight kissed her hand. The knight marveled at the jewels upon her delicate fingers. The knight spoke nice gentlemanly words to her. The whole time, though, the princess was not looking at the knight. It was the boy who had caught the princess's eye. And it was the boy who fell deeply, instantly in love with her.

In the great hall that night, with much pomp and ceremony, the king issued the challenge to bring the single ear of barley from the North, and the knight accepted. And behind them, shy glances and secret smiles were given and received. Both knight and page lay in bed later, happily unable to sleep, though for very different reasons.

In the morning, as the knight and his page left the castle, the knight smiled and waved to the crowd that had gathered in the courtyard. The page was also smiling and waving—to a small figure in a high window, silently wishing him well on his way.

When they were within a day's ride of the northern mountains where the giant lived, the boy asked, "How will you succeed where so many others have failed?"

The knight replied confidently, "I have travelled here before and spent many weeks secretly watching the giant. He has kept to the same routine longer than any man can remember.

"For seven days and nights he works his grain field without rest. On the evening of the seventh day, he grinds a large hill of barley between two flat stones, each stone the size of a farmer's field. Then he fills a huge sack with the ground meal.

"He makes three massive cakes from the leftover barley meal and puts them down into a smoking mountain to bake. Then he throws his sack of meal over his shoulder, leaves his valley and crosses the foothills to the village. There, he calls upon the local miller, to whom he sells his meal for three large coins of gold.

"His business done at the miller's, he proceeds to the village inn and orders a vast quantity of the 'stoutest stout,' as he calls it. The innkeeper brings the beer in huge vats, each the size of a house. The giant pours the contents of every one of these into his mouth before swallowing the whole lot at once.

"He then returns to the mountains for his supper of barley cakes and when he is done, he takes out his pipes. Though I have heard the tune as clear as my own voice, I cannot say I've observed his playing. It is said the one huge breath he draws is enough to let him play for the whole evening without stopping. When he is finally out of breath, he lays down his pipes and sleeps straight through for another seven days."

The knight smiled smugly. "The others who wanted to steal an ear of the giant's barley did not use their heads. They all thought the best time was either when the giant was away in the village or sound asleep. Each time, the giant heard them pulling down his barley and snapping it from its stalk. It is my intention to take the barley when the giant begins playing his pipes. I will use their noise to mask the sound of the breaking stalk. And," the knight added, smoothing his moustaches, "I will have the next seven days when he is snoring to escape."

The boy said nothing, fearing the knight's anger. But in his heart of hearts he felt this plan was as surely doomed as all the others had been.

They plodded on until sunset, and reached the little village inn where the giant drank his beer. When they woke from a good sound sleep the next morning, the knight bought a cart that he planned to use to transport the monstrous ear of barley, once he'd stolen it. That night they crossed the foothills of the mountains, not wanting to be seen by the giant on the broad, treeless hills during the day.

The closer they got to the giant's field in the mountain valley, the louder came the sound of the giant at work. At first the boy thought the thunderous sound was some huge waterfall or rushing river. It echoed from the cliffs and the ground shook beneath their feet, making the horses uneasy. When the two crept over the final ridge to look down on the huge grain field and the giant at work, the boy at once understood the source of the sound.

The giant, the boy now saw, was not quite as tall as the clouds. He was crouched in his field, weeding with his bare hands. The weeds, though, were not mere thistles or couch grass. They were huge fir and pine trees, each one as thick as a barrel and a hundred feet high. The barley stalks towered over the trees, at least three times their height. The giant was gouging out the trees in bunches and pitching them up the mountainside as if they were tufts of grass. Every once in a while the giant would stand up and stretch. He was three times again as tall as his grain and stood well over the height of the ridge where the knight and boy hid. Then he'd crouch back to work and the thunder of his massive hands gouging the rocky ground would resume.

At first the boy was filled with wonder. When he thought of actually going down the mountainside and trying to steal an ear of the giant's barley, his heart sank.

If the giant noticed his grain was missing, even days later, how could they hope to get away from this place?

On the way back down the ridge to make a camp for the night, he couldn't help but say to the knight, "Your life will be in great peril. After seeing that valley, I'm afraid our journey is going to end very badly."

His master gave him a cutting look. "Our journey will end only when I marry that princess and begin spending the king's gold," he said. "I will not leave here without that barley. Now speak no more of it."

They had been camped for three nights before the giant's week of work ended. And then there was no mistaking what was happening. The event was announced to the valley and sky by the thunderous roar of the giant pulling barley from the ground by the handful. When he had a heap nearly half as high as the surrounding mountains, he broke the ears from the stalks, and rubbed them between his hands till the chaff fell away. Then he blew the chaff into the next country till all that was left were beautiful, big pearls of barley.

The giant turned and reached into a far valley and brought over two huge flat stones. He spent the next hour grinding the hill of grain into meal. Then it took nearly as long for the giant to fill his huge sack. He kept adding a pinch here and taking away a pinch there. The boy saw that the giant was so precise in his weighing of the sack that he measured down to the very grains. He'd blow a bit of dust off the top or let a grain or two drop into the sack from the swirling grooves of a fingertip.

Finally, he was satisfied with the weight of the massive sack. Scooping up the barley meal that remained on the ground, he made three huge cakes by mixing the meal with water he got from a nearby river and patted them flat. He put the cakes deep into the mouth of a smoking mountain to bake. Then after blowing on the fires inside to bring them to life, he hefted the sack of meal to his shoulder.

When the giant turned their way, the boy's heart leapt in his chest, for in three strides he was upon them and in another stride he had stepped over the mountain ridge where they were camped. It wasn't fear or wonder that charged the boy's heart at the giant's passing, but a sharp stroke of pity. For as the giant strode overhead the boy saw that the giant's hands were covered in blood, scratched and nicked from the harsh work of weeding his field.

The next moment, after ordering the boy to keep watch, the knight went racing down the slope to ready the cart and horses.

The foothills that had taken them ten hours to cross, the giant went over in a few steps. He arrived at the village while the miller and innkeeper were still scrambling to be ready for the giant's arrival.

"Miller!" the giant shouted as he stepped into the village.

Ready or not, the miller immediately appeared in the street before him, wringing his straw hat in his hands. "Y-yes, kind sir."

"Miller! I have brought you ten and twenty thousand bushels of the finest meal. My trade is honest and my pockets are empty."

The miller bowed, and saluted, and tried to form his mouth into a welcoming smile instead of a grimace of terror. All the while, he nervously gestured to his two sons, who stood in the doorway of the mill house. The sons slowly rolled out a gold coin the size of a cartwheel and let it thump down in the middle of the street. They hurried back for two more and with great difficulty lifted each one atop the first. That done, the miller and his sons scrambled into the mill house and fought to shut the door as quickly as they could.

The giant gently set his huge sack of meal in the street, making the mill house look like a dollhouse beside it. As gently as it seemed to touch the ground, the heavy whomp of it still made a few chimney pots tumble off of the village roofs. Reaching down, the giant picked up the three coins between his fingers and straightened, eyeing them carefully. Satisfied, he dropped them into a bag tied to his belt and took one big step down the street to the village inn.

"Innkeeper!" the giant shouted through his parched lips.

The innkeeper appeared in the street as quickly as he could. "Y-yes, kind sir."

"Innkeeper! Bring me ten and twenty thousand pints of your stoutest stout! My mouth is dry and my gold is good!"

With the help of most of the men and women of the little village, the innkeeper got all the barrels of beer together on the road in front of his inn. When that was done, he shouted up to the giant, "Ten and twenty thousand pints of the stoutest stout for you, kind sir!" Then, like a mouse before a looming cat, the innkeeper scurried down to his cellar with his helpers and shut the door.

The giant lifted one barrel after another as if they were thimbles and poured the beer into his mouth. When he'd emptied all the barrels into his mouth and shaken them to make sure they were dry, a strange expression came over his face. He swallowed the beer in a single gulp, and wiped his mouth with the back of his hand. "Innkeeper!" the giant shouted in a rage. "Innkeeper!"

The poor innkeeper came rushing from his cellar, blinded both by the light and by his terror. "K-kind sir," he managed to stammer, "is something wrong?"

"Innkeeper, you were two drops shy this day."

The innkeeper did not know where to look. He was wringing the apron in his hands to shreds and his knees quivered like saplings in a breeze. "I am truly sorry, but that is all the good stout we could make this time."

"Never!" shouted the giant, blowing roof tiles down the street. "Never let it happen again."

Then, reaching into the bag tied to his belt, he took out the three gold pieces and tossed them near the innkeeper. Two of the coins stuck fast in the ground. The third one tripped up the innkeeper and buried itself in the wall of the inn. "It was the finest stout, nonetheless," said the giant, with just the hint of a smile.

Turning, he made his way back to his mountain valley for his supper.

The moment the boy saw the giant returning, he signalled frantically to his master. The knight had thrown ropes around the shortest stalk of barley and was tying them to the harness of the two horses. The horses were wild-eyed and fretting, for the ground was shaking with the footsteps of the approaching giant.

Crouched low among the rocks, the boy watched the giant pass above him, striding over the ridge to where his cakes were baking. Dropping to one knee, the giant dipped a hand into the smoking mountain to check his supper—then froze when one of the horses whinnied. The giant frowned. Then stood. And the stalk of barley suddenly broke with a resounding *crack* that echoed through the valley.

The horses stumbled and screamed to get out from under the crashing barley stalk and the tangle of ropes. As the giant's angry footfalls shook the mountain, the horses ran for their lives, dragging the cart off to who-knows-where.

The giant stood over the knight and his broken stalk of barley. The knight had barely gotten two words out to plead for his life when the giant reached down and silenced the knight by driving him into the ground with his finger. Then he brushed a little soil over the spot and without so much as the twitch of an eyebrow, he stomped off to check his baking barley cakes again.

The boy, frightened out of his mind, slid madly down the ridge and found a hiding place in a dense grove of trees. He dared not move. Hours upon hours passed without a sound. It was as if even the birds were too afraid to chirp. The sunlight left the hills. A slight breeze came up that chilled the boy to the marrow. Then, in the gathering darkness came the sound of the giant groaning with happiness over his dinner as the toasted smell of the barley cakes drifted for miles.

The boy lay shivering in the grove, too afraid to flee in the darkness, too distraught to sleep. As the moon began to rise, the giant picked up his pipes and started playing the merriest jig the boy had ever heard. The sweet music echoed around the hills.

The boy could not have said how he fell asleep. In the morning, the deep snoring of the giant woke him, rumbling through the ground beneath him like an earth-quake. He crept carefully to the bottom of the ridge, spent the day crossing the foothills and arrived in the village in the early evening, relieved and footsore.

The moment he entered the main street, people began pointing and exclaiming. A minute later, a small crowd formed and two strong lads boosted him onto their shoulders.

"What is this? What's going on?" he exclaimed.

The innkeeper came out into the street from beside his inn. He was followed by two men leading horses. "Aren't these your horses? And look, isn't this your cart and barley?"

The boy's eyes went wide. There, beside the inn, stood the cart the knight had bought. And behind it was the ear of barley, which had been dragged behind in a tangle of ropes. "Um… yes!" he answered. "I believe it is!"

"My cousin found the horses up in his field yesterday," said the innkeeper. "We know all about that challenge. Where so many have failed, you are the first person to come back alive from those mountains with the prize."

The boy thanked the innkeeper and spent the night in his inn. The next morning, with the distant rumble of the giant's snores still echoing from the mountains, the boy climbed into the cart, not quite believing his good fortune. Even if it was only by luck, the fact remained that he was the only one who had ever completed this first supposedly impossible task set by the king.

All the way back to the castle, he couldn't stop sighing, thinking of the princess. When he arrived, though, he didn't get the reception he'd expected, despite the fact that he told the story as truthfully as it had happened. Yes, the common people cheered him and the princess could not contain her excitement at his arrival. But the king threw a dark pall over his success by accusing him of killing the knight and stealing the prize for himself.

Everyone at court wondered if the king would even consider the first task complete. The king had issued the challenge to the knight, not his page. While the common people of the town rioted outside the castle gates, wanting the king to believe the page, the boy was left in the back kitchen with the servants to eat a cold supper while the king met with his counsellors to decide what to do.

For five hours they argued over the problem. Finally the princess entered the council chamber and stood to one side, arms crossed, glaring at her father. The king and his counsellors hummed and hawed for another half-hour, examining the problem from every side. Then at midnight, the king reached a decision: the boy would be allowed to continue. It was said there was only one reason why the king gave in. He couldn't bear to have his daughter standing there staring at him like that. Though he wouldn't dare admit it.

So the next morning the boy entered the throne room, which was richly decorated for the revealing of the last three impossible tasks. The queen wanted nothing to do with the proceedings, but all of the counsellors were present, clad in fine robes and seated in gilt chairs. Everyone who was anyone crammed into the throne room to see this stripling boy addressed by the king. The boy knelt before the king's dais. The princess was beside her father and her eyes never left the handsome youth.

"Rise, boy," the king commanded. "We have decided," he glanced sidelong at his daughter, "to accept that you have completed the first task."

One of the counsellors handed the king a leather pouch, which he in turn held out to the boy. "For your effort, you have earned this pouch of gold. You are free to keep it and walk away and never set foot in this castle again. This gold is both to reward you and to encourage you to leave. For," he said in a much louder voice, "let it be known that if you fail any of the final three tasks, there will be no second chance to win my daughter's favour. You will be banished from the kingdom and never see this castle, the princess, or your own family ever again. No attempt at contact will be tolerated."

A great rumbling rose from the crowd, half of them exclaiming and the other half hushing them because they wanted to hear.

"Despite my wishes," said the king, "my daughter has said she will consider you—and only you—as a suitor for her hand in marriage, should you succeed. But before I reveal the last three tasks, are you willing to take up this great challenge?"

With a pounding heart, the boy tried to find his voice. All he could think of was his father, and how he'd promised to help him in his old age. If he were banished, there would be no hope of that. He looked up at the princess. Her smile seemed to encourage him, though the fearful look in her eyes made his heart pound all the more. He thought the boring life he had left behind, the endless hours making charcoal and hammering till his arms ached. And he knew that it was for just such a challenge that he had left home.

So he plucked up his courage and replied, more to the princess than to the king, "I accept the challenge, Your Majesty."

The people in the throne room cheered and clapped loudly, for it seemed everyone wanted the boy to succeed.

The king pushed the curls of his moustache to each side, obviously disappointed at this brash boy who insisted on pushing on. "So be it," he said. "You have accepted the challenge and I will now reveal the final three tasks."

The crowd fell deathly silent, waiting.

"Boy, there is a lake about a mile from the castle walls that we call the Lake of the Endless Beach. It takes four men rowing a small boat a full day to cross this lake, and seven days for any man to walk around it. The beach around this lake is very wide and those who have taken sand from it assure me they have never dug so deep that they have reached anything but more sand. It is your first task to count the sand of this beach, one grain at a time, and report to me your exact count when you are done."

The crowd gasped. The boy, losing all hope of accomplishing the task, sank to his knees in horror.

"The second task," said the king in a commanding tone, "is to count every drop of water in the Lake of the Endless Beach and report the exact count to me when you are done."

The boy's head swam with the impossibility of such a task. He fell forward, bracing himself with his hands on the marble floor. The crowd buzzed with astonishment.

"Silence!" shouted the king. The crowd fell quiet. "The final task will bring you to the woodland on the southern side of the lake. This place is known as the Dark Forest. It is so densely wooded that the many branches block all sunlight from reaching the ground. The forest is so vast, it takes a full six weeks to ride around its perimeter. It is your final task to count every leaf of every tree in this forest and report the exact number to me when you are done. Your success will make you sole suitor for my daughter's hand; failure, your complete banishment."

Without so much as a glance at the crowd, the king gathered his robes around him and strode from the hall.

The moment he was gone, the voices of the crowd rose to a fevered pitch. To the boy, the voices were a meaningless buzz. His head was swimming. He didn't know if he should run from the hall in shame, or fall in a faint where he knelt. *They may as well throw me out of the kingdom or bury me alive right now,* he thought. For he felt at that moment that his failure was as certain as the impossibility of the tasks that had been set for him.

Two court guards lifted him to his feet. As they walked him from the hall, he looked back to see the distressed princess being comforted by her ladies-in-waiting. But she peeked past her maids and tried to give him an encouraging smile as the guards led him away.

The king had given him a small room off the castle kitchen in which to spend the night, but the princess persuaded one of the courtiers to give up his room for the boy. Now he lay in the richest, softest bed he had ever been in, unable to sleep. He thought of the tasks, saved from despair only by memory of the princess's encouraging smile.

His thoughts turned to the knight and the giant of the North. Everyone had thought the first task was impossible. Three dozen good men, the knight had said, had failed to get the ear of barley. Yet he himself, a poor smith's son, was the one who had—apparently—succeeded. Over and over in his mind, he asked himself, *Why?* Was there a reason? Or was it pure luck?

Eventually, he drifted off to sleep. But in the wee hours, he dreamed that he was killed by a giant, over and over again, each death more horrible than the last. He woke from each dream in a sweat, trembling with fear. Looming failure haunted him. How many lifetimes would it take to count every grain of sand on the beach, every drop of water in the lake and every leaf in the forest?

Just as morning broke and the first rays of sunlight pierced his room, he decided to flee the castle. Tucking the leather pouch full of gold in his belt, he tried the door and found it unlocked. But when he opened it, two pole-axes came down to cross in front of him, and the guards holding them commanded he return to his room.

The boy went to the window and slumped against its stone frame, barely able to keep back his tears. As he stood there, his eyes fell upon three gardeners outside, arriving to work on the king's flowerbeds and lawns. As they set to work, he thought of the many times he had made rakes and shovels just like theirs, back in his father's shop. He could see from here that the ones he made were much better. And he gave a sorrowful laugh, thinking, *I would have been better off staying at home, pounding out shovel blades.*

It was right then that an idea came to him. He stood. As his tears dried in the early morning sun, he was not thinking of the impossibility of the tasks before him. He was thinking how someone, perhaps the king himself, had laid out all the pieces as clear as day. It only remained to fit them together to accomplish each task in turn, with the ease of raking a garden.

Returning to the door, this time he knocked before opening it. Again the poleaxes came down, but the boy said, "Put your weapons aside, for I am ready to attempt the tasks."

The guards lifted their poleaxes and stepped aside. They followed the boy along the hallway and down the wide marble stairs.

"Summon the king," he said to one of them when he'd reached the bottom. "I will await him here."

It was some time before the king could be roused out of bed. Finally, the boy saw him descending the great staircase with the princess behind him, her long hair in braids. The boy stood his ground and waited.

When the king approached, the boy knelt on one knee before him and said, "Your Majesty, I ask leave to begin the noble tasks you have set me. But I must be free to go where I please so I can prepare myself."

"Leave is granted," the king said, "though these guards will stay by your side until the tasks are complete."

"That is fine. And thank you, Your Majesty," said the boy, rising.

The boy strode out into the fresh morning air, the guards with their poleaxes behind him. Days later, the boy and his two guards arrived at the foothills of the mountains of the North.

But on hearing the giant's deafening snores, the guards dropped their poleaxes and ran off, leaving the boy alone.

For the next three days, the boy worked hard, putting his plan into action.

When his work was done, he pulled a large rock over himself to make it appear he was caught. Then he began shouting, "Help! Help! Is there anyone near who can help me! Help!"

It wasn't long before the giant heard the plea from the other side of the ridge. He was still rubbing his eyes after his long sleep when he stepped close to where the boy lay.

"I am down here and I am caught fast! Help me!" the boy called up to him.

When the giant knelt down to see what was the matter, the boy feared that was the end of him. For under the giant's knees the trees cracked and slapped down around him like massive whips.

"What is this?" the giant asked, flicking the rock off the boy as if it were a grain of sand. "And what are you doing in my mountains?"

The boy pointed to the pile of wood and rock he had spent the last three days constructing. "This is to be a furnace, good sir," he said to the giant. "For I am a smith and would like to help you in your need."

The giant sat up and bellowed down to the boy, "I need nothing, little man."

"Ah, but you do. I can clearly see the scrapes and scars upon your hands from your hard work. I am skilled at making tools that will spare your hands. When you take up your pipes, there will be no blood to mar them."

This caught the giant's interest. Though he was still very suspicious of this tiny intruder., "How do I know you are not a thief, like so many others who have come here before?"

"Good sir," said the boy, "I am no thief. I am a simple soul who earns his keep by the work of his hands, like you. As you can see, I have come by the light of day to make an honest trade. I will make tools for you if you agree to help me. I am no thief."

The giant scowled down at the tiny boy for a moment. Then he burst into laughter. "Little man, I admire your pluck. But how can you make a tool large enough to be of any use to me?"

"I was trying to build a forge here with these rocks when one fell on top of me. I fear it will be many weeks before it can be finished. If only there were some quicker way to build a large forge…"

"I could help you," said the giant. "And there is no need to build a forge. For your purposes, that smoking mountain would surely do far better."

So a pact was made. The giant willingly helped the young smith with his work, eager for the tools the boy promised him. The giant dug ore from the mountain and followed the boy's every direction to the letter. In three days' time, they'd finished making a huge sickle, a fine great hoe and a shovel so large, the boy couldn't throw a stone far enough to reach across the blade. When he tried the new tools in the field, the giant was so pleased with them that he put the boy up on his shoulder and carried him down to the village for as much of the 'stoutest stout' as he could drink.

The next morning, the boy awoke to find the giant standing beside him, waiting to fulfill his part of their bargain.

Ten minutes later the boy was riding on the giant's shoulder back to the kingdom where the tasks were to take place. The journey that had taken several days by horse took the giant but a few dozen strides. When they arrived, people were just getting out of bed and making their breakfast. Though when they saw the giant coming, they dropped their breakfast on the floor and ran to hide under their beds.

The giant had a good look at the Lake of the Endless Beach. Then he crouched down and talked with the boy for some time. A short while later, they were back at the giant's mountains.

Beyond the valley where the giant grew his barley lay a heap of meal bags that the boy had thought was a mountain itself. The giant shooed a few goats from the heap before scooping up an armload of the bags. Then off they went to the Lake of the Endless Beach, the giant with the boy on his shoulder, the meal bags under one arm and his new shovel under the other.

Over the whole afternoon and evening, the giant filled the bags with sand. While the boy slept, the giant kept working through the night. He made little waves in the lake with his finger so the last sands would be washed ashore and the waters of the lake would rest on bare rock. In the morning, the boy helped collect the last grains of sand. These were swept into the giant's shovel and poured into the last bag.

By this time a great crowd had gathered. The boy heard whispers that the king himself was on his way.

The boy called for a pen and ink and a hundred pieces of parchment. While they waited for the parchment to come, the boy took up a piece of coal and, as the giant told him the number of grains in each bag, he wrote the numbers down on the bare rock of the beach to add them up. Though the giant knew his weights and measures, he knew nothing of writing.

When the hundred pieces of parchment arrived, some of the local people helped the boy stitch them together. Then he took up the quill pen, dipped it in the ink and began to write the long, long number of the grains of sand from the Lake of the Endless Beach. It took him from late morning till mid-afternoon to write out the number.

By then, the king had come down to the lake with all his counsellors in their fancy robes trailing behind him, to see the giant and watch the goings-on. The boy rolled up the hundred pieces of parchment and presented the scroll to the king.

The king handed the parchment to his counsellors, who proceeded to unroll it. They examined it carefully from up close and far away, right side up and upside down. The boy began to get worried as they hummed and hawed and whispered among themselves. Finally, the king returned to the boy with the parchment scroll and said, "How can you prove that this is the right number?"

The boy stood dazed for a moment. Then he looked up at the giant, whose cheeks were beginning to redden.

"Wait!" said the giant in a voice that shook the crowd where they stood. And he strode off.

He was back in three minutes with one of his fists full of men and women. He set them down before the king with a thump. "Tell him," growled the giant.

It was the miller from the village near the giant's mountains, with all the people who worked the giant's meal.

When the miller had recovered his breath and courage from being carried across the countryside, he said, "Since my father's time and my father's father's time and so long before that no one can remember, this man has come to my mill house every other week with ten and twenty thousand bushels of meal. Not once in a hundred years has he been over or under this amount, not by a fleck of dust. I would stake my life on his count."

"And so would I," came the voice of another man from the village.

"And so would I," said all the people who helped sort the ten and twenty thousand bushels.

The king rubbed his moustache and said, "Well, I don't know..."

The giant reached down and picked up the king by a pinch of his robes, and bellowed in his face, "You doubt the word of these fine people?"

"No, no—" the king sputtered. "I-I declare this task successfully completed! Now put me down!"

The giant, under the pleas of the boy and the crowd behind him, reluctantly set the king back upon the ground.

"Your Majesty is very kind," said the boy. "I promise an exact count for the final two tasks, as well."

The boy looked up to the giant, who was still red-faced at the king's insult. "Are you ready for the next task?"

"I am at your service," said the giant as calmly as he could.

The king and the entire crowd backed away from the lake at the giant's bidding. The giant set the boy upon his shoulder once more, lifted his shovel and walked out into the countryside. Setting the boy down, he began digging a huge pit. When he was done, the pit was miles long and as deep as a mountain canyon.

Then he got down on his hands and knees over the lake. He gave the boy a grin and proceeded to slurp up water and swish it around in his mouth a moment. Then he spat the water into the pit he had dug with an enormous spray, which soaked anyone who was nearby. He told the boy how much water he had slurped and went back for more. The boy called for parchment and wrote the numbers till late into the evening. When it was dark, he was given a lamp to see by, for the giant kept working, all through the night.

Late in the afternoon of the next day, the boy had the king and his counsellors summoned, for the lake was completely dry. He worked at the numbers on the parchment, adding them up, while the giant stood over him, watching.

"Thirty-one and a half billion, six hundred and eleven thousand, twenty-one and a quarter pints," he declared. "Plus six drops."

The king accepted the parchment from him and passed it on to his counsellors, who examined it up close and far away, right side up and upside down. They hummed and hawed and whispered among themselves for a long while. Finally, the king took the rolled-up parchment and said, "Is there anyone here who can assure me this count is true?"

"Wait!" said the giant, and in three minutes he was back with another fistful of people from the village near his home. This time it was the innkeeper and all his helpers.

"Tell him," the giant bellowed.

The innkeeper, hardly recovered from his ride, said, "Since my father's time and my father's father's time and so long before that no one can remember, this...rather large man has come to my inn every other week and ordered ten and twenty thousand pints of the stoutest stout. If ever I was over by a drop or a drop shy, he was able to tell immediately. I would stake my life on his count."

"And so would I," came the voice of a woman behind him.

"And so would I," said another dozen people from the innkeeper's village.

The king rubbed his moustaches. He was about to say something, then changed his mind when he saw the giant's shadow loom over him. "Yes, yes," he said so everyone could hear. "I declare this task successfully completed! No need to be upset."

"Now for the final task," said the boy. To the giant he said, "Are you ready?"

"As ever I will be," growled the giant, still angry with the king. He lifted the boy to his shoulder and strode around the lake to the edge of the Dark Forest.

There, he crouched down on all fours and took in a breath that would have played his pipes for seven nights straight. Then he began to blow. And blow. And blow.

The wind from his lungs sent king, counsellors, courtiers and townspeople tumbling like dust balls back toward the castle. Twenty-three of the castle guards were ordered to stand behind the king so he wouldn't be blown away.

The giant blew steadily till near sunset. When he was done, the giant stomped back to where the king stood and set the boy down before him. Now that the wind had stopped, a huge crowd came from the town and castle and stood silently waiting.

"Your Majesty," said the boy. "I have the exact count of the number of leaves on the trees in the whole of the Dark Forest."

The king couldn't help a wry smile. "And what might that number be?"

"Your Majesty," the boy answered, "there are but two leaves left on the trees of the Dark Forest."

The huge crowd burst into laughter and loud cheering and whistling. The king sent some of the counsellors across the lake to confirm that this was true—though no one was willing to wait till they came back with their answer.

The king laid a hand on the boy's shoulder and said, "My lad, I cannot deny the truth of your count." To the crowd he said, "I declare the four tasks successfully completed!"

A cheer went up that was like no other in the history of the kingdom. The king and all his counsellors had to plug their ears. Hats flew into the air, trumpets blared and the people hoisted the boy up onto their shoulders.

The princess had been watching from the castle walls and the crowd parted and fell silent as she approached.

"My daughter," said the king, "will you have this lad for a suitor?"

The people set the boy down and everyone jostled to see the princess and hear her answer. She waited till the boy had come to stand in front of her. Then she looked at the king and said, "Indeed I will, Father."

Well, if the cheer that went up before was loud, this one was deafening. The giant found the sound extremely annoying and went to dump out the sacks of sand along the lakeshore, and refill the lake and the huge pit he had dug. When he was done, he waved his shovel in the air to get the boy's attention. Since the clouds overhead went skittering off in all directions from the shovel, the boy noticed at once.

"It was a pleasure doing an honest trade with you," the giant called. And before the boy could thank him, off the giant went, striding back over the countryside to his mountains in the North.

The boy was invited to stay in the castle so the princess could get to know him. As it turned out, they became the best of friends and were rarely seen apart. Within the year, it was announced they were to be married and no happier couple was to be found in all the kingdom.

"Well," asked the king one day of his queen, "are you happy with this lad as your daughter's betrothed?"

Over the past year, the queen had been quite taken with the boy, noting his hard work and good manners. But that was not all. "I have to admit," she said, "I haven't had a single argument with our girl since he came to stay with us. All is repaired. And I have to tell you, he is so handsome, I cry a little bit with happiness every time I think of how beautiful our grandchildren are going to be."

The boy sent a messenger to his father with the bag of gold he had been saving since completing the first task. He told his father to sell everything and come stay with him in the castle, where he could retire in peace and comfort.

No wedding in memory was fancier than this one. A massive feast was laid out in the great hall, which was draped with garlands from one end to the other. The giant was invited and sat outside on the huge bags of barley meal he had brought as a wedding gift for the couple. The king had arranged for the giant to be served a hundred thousand pints of the stoutest stout, which put the giant in a merry mood.

At the table, the two fathers loudly joked and told stories about their children, who turned away and pretended to ignore them. By the end of the meal the two were fast friends, and the king said to the boy's father, "If you ever want something to keep you busy, the royal blacksmith shop could use your skill."

But the boy's father said, "Oh, no. I'm old now and I only want peace and quiet for my remaining years."

The newlyweds went off to the king's summer house for their honeymoon. When they returned two weeks later, they boy was surprised to find his father out back of the castle, with twenty or thirty men all following his orders. He wore shining new boots. His white hair was cropped close. And on his face was a huge smile.

"Father," said the boy. "What are you doing? I thought you were tired and wanted nothing but peace and quiet in your old age."

His father replied, "I took the king up on his offer. I'm now in charge of the armoury, the stables and everything else outside here. Every day I get to do something new and interesting. I learned that lesson from you, my boy. After all, there is nothing worse than being bored."

The Sneaking Girl

and the Other Queen

The Sneaking Girl and the Other Queen

There was once a woman who had three lovely daughters. They lived in a little house by a bog and the woman earned her living by sewing and weaving. When her first girl was old enough, the mother showed her all the tricks of working a needle and thread. "You're so quick," she told her daughter. "I only have to show you once and you can do it." The two would sit on either side of the fireplace and make the finest quilts out of scraps from the rag box.

When the next girl was old enough, her mother took her down to the bog to collect reeds and showed her how to weave baskets from them. "You're just as quick as your sister," the mother told her. "No need to show you a thing more than once." So the girl would sit weaving between her mother and sister, setting her finished baskets on the hearth to dry.

But when it came time to show the third girl how to make things, the mother was tired of children by then and didn't bother. "There's no more room around the fire," she said. "Go somewhere else and be quiet."

The girl had nothing else to do, so she would sneak around the house and try not to get caught. When she was very lonely she would try to get her sisters' attention by jumping out from unexpected places.

"Can't you be useful?" said the eldest when the girl startled her and made her break her thread.

"Sneaking," added the middle sister. "That's all you're good at. Maybe when you're older you can get a job sneaking."

Since their little house was near the bog, every year it sank a little deeper into the ground. Sadly, this was the mother's undoing, for one winter day, she cracked her head on the low door and never got up again.

As time passed and the house sank too low for the eldest girl, she decided she would go off to seek her fortune. "I shall be Queen of Rags!" she declared. And off she went to the little village nearby, where she sold her quilts to anyone who would buy them. But after only one month, she followed her mother to the grave when she pricked her finger with a needle and it wouldn't stop bleeding.

After a while the house sank even deeper into the bog and the middle child found it too much trouble to get in and out through the door. So off she went to seek her fortune. "I shall be Queen of Reeds!" she declared. She followed her sister to the little village nearby and made a good living making and selling her baskets. But after two months, she went to collect reeds one day and got stuck in the mucky shore of a big lake and drowned.

Now alone, the youngest girl was fine for a little while, crawling in and out through the low door. But soon enough, there was no house left to crawl into. With no hope of making anything to sell, she thought she would go to the village to find work. The next morning, that's what she did and set off across the countryside with nothing more than one poor dress and her head to stick out of it.

When she arrived, she went down the village's one narrow street, looking into all the open doors to see what people were doing. If she liked it, she thought, perhaps she could ask for a job there. But at the fishmonger's she thought it smelled stinky, so she passed it by. At the baker's it smelled quite wonderful, but the baker's hands were covered in scars from oven burns, and she didn't like that at all.

Nothing appealed to her until she came to a small house at a bend in the street. There, an old woman was sitting behind her window, selling the ugliest clay cups the girl had ever seen. *Well,* she thought, *anybody can make cups as ugly as those.* So she asked the old woman if she might work for her.

"And why should I hire you?" the old woman asked her.

"Well," said the girl, "I am very quick. Just show me once and I can do it."

"Fine," said the old woman, and invited the girl inside. She sat the girl up on the tall stool by the open window and stood over her. "Here's how it will go. For the first year, I need you to sit at the window and sell the cups I make. If you don't sit still, you're of no use to me, and I'll throw you out in the street like dishwater. In the second year, I'll bring you clay and you can knead it to prepare it for me while you wait for customers. But again, if you don't work hard, you're of no use to me, and I'll throw you out like dishwater."

"That doesn't sound very good," said the girl.

The old woman ignored her. "In the third year, I'll bring out my potter's wheel and you can watch me make my cups. And if you don't keep a sharp eye, you're of no use to me, so—"

"Wait," said the girl. "Three years and I still haven't made a single cup?"

"Oh," said the old woman, "they are very difficult to make. It takes time."

The girl rolled her eyes and looked out the door, thinking, *Surely there is somewhere better to make a living.*

"I will feed you one bite of bread and one bite of fish every day," the old woman told her.

"Is that all?" The girl sighed deeply.

"And you can sleep on the hearth there when it gets cold."

"Ugh," said the girl.

"One more thing," the old woman told her. "You see that curtain in the back of the house? You may never pass that curtain," she warned, wagging a bony finger in the girl's face, "or it's dishwater for you."

The girl sat there for a moment, squinting up at the old woman. "That seems like a lot of trouble," she said, and she jumped down off the stool. "So no, thank you. I think I will be on my way."

Two skips and a hop later, the girl was back outside, glad to be out of that crazy old woman's house. *I can't wait three years just to make ugly cups,* she thought. *And that curtain? That's much too tempting. I'd be sneaking behind that on the first day!*

So the girl got out onto the high road, wondering where she could go. Her sisters wanted to be Queen of Rags and Queen of Reeds. With no hope of being queen of anything, perhaps she could go to the real queen's castle and find work. So she trudged on and a few days later she arrived at the queen's castle. She knew enough to go around to the back where the servants were and knocked hard on the big door.

A girl not much older than her answered the door. She was called the drudge, as she did all the dirty, tiresome jobs in the kitchen, like scrubbing burnt pots and wiping up spills. The drudge only had one thing to say to the girl: "What are you good at?"

"Well…nothing right now," the girl answered.

The drudge gave a snort and started to close the door on her.

"Wait! Wait!" said the girl. "I can do anything you ask. And I am very quick. Just show me once and I can do it."

The drudge rolled her eyes. "Well, that would be a fine trick, if it's true. But you'll have to prove it." And she pulled the girl inside. The drudge took her down a narrow hall at the very back of the kitchen and put her into a small room with nothing more than a straw bed, a spinning wheel and a little sewing box.

After a while the drudge returned with a pot holder that had a tiny red crown on it, to say it was from the queen's kitchen. "Here," said the drudge, who didn't mind teasing the girl. "See if you can make that." And she showed her quick and out she ran with the pot holder, banging the door shut behind her.

The girl looked at the door and the sad little bed and the spinning wheel. *Now I've got myself in a fix,* she thought. *How can I make a pot holder, just like that? I can't even remember what it looked like!*

She pulled some straw from her bed and tried putting it in the spinning wheel. But the straw just flew around the room and made a mess. Then she found the needle and thread in the sewing box, but after a few minutes of trying to thread the needle, she got a pain in her left eye and gave up. What was she to do?

After a little while, she opened the door a crack and looked out. There was no one around, so she went sneaking from doorway to doorway until she came to the kitchen where the drudge worked. And there, hanging by the fire, was the pot holder she was supposed to copy. Quick as a wink, she snatched it up and hurried back to her room, hoping to get a better look at it so she could figure out how to make one.

But the moment she was back on her bed, the drudge returned with a cup of water and a piece of bread. "What have you done?" the drudge exclaimed. "Here I was, bringing you some food and drink, and you've already finished your task! You truly are quick and able to make a thing after only one look at it." And before the girl could say a word, the drudge rushed out with the pot holder to show the cook.

The cook was mightily impressed and through the course of the day, the story of the pot holder made its way around the castle. The cook showed the hall boy and the hall boy showed the maids and soon all the servants in the castle knew about it. Before long, even the queen noticed the commotion in the hall outside the library where she was working.

The queen was a very royal looking person with a high white wig and a gown that went on forever. She was in the midst of a very important meeting with her mayors, ministers and magistrates. She did not like being disturbed when she was working and sent her chamberlain out to see what the noise was.

The chamberlain was the one who enforced the rules for being proper and correct. He was in charge of all the other servants and if you didn't do what he said, you'd end up in the dungeon with the skeletons, starving in the dark. "What's going on out here?" he asked the servants in the hall.

They told him about the pot holder and how the new kitchen girl, who was even lower than a drudge, had made it in a few minutes.

"Ridiculous!" he said. "Now get away from the door and be quiet."

"What was all that about?" asked the queen when he returned.

The chamberlain reported that a girl in the kitchen, a drudge's helper, had made a pot holder in just a few minutes and all the servants were amazed.

"Well, let's see this amazing thing," said the queen.

So the chamberlain went out and had the hall boy bring the pot holder from the kitchen.

"It's nicely done," said the queen. "But it is only a pot holder, after all. Give her something more challenging to do and tell the servants to quiet down. I'll never get to the seaside if I don't finish this."

The queen had been talking of going to the seaside for a long time. A very long time. When she was a little girl and her father, the king, was alive, he took her there on holiday and they played on the beach. She remembered the boats bobbing in the bay and in the evening, far out over the water, the sun rolling off the edge of the sea like a great big pearl. She dreamt of going back there one day, when all her work was done. The trouble was, her work was never done.

The chamberlain wanted nothing more than to keep the queen happy. It was a simple matter to find something more challenging for the girl to make. So he went straight up the stairs to see the royal dresser. She was quite an old woman who had been the young queen's governess and now took care of her majesty's wardrobe and wigs, brushing and tidying, and helping the queen get ready in the morning.

The dresser understood the problem immediately. She went to the queen's cupboard and fetched a very beautiful scarf, which had a crane embroidered on it. "See if the girl can do that. But make sure you bring it back after, as it's one of the queen's favourites. It was brought from far across the desert by the great master merchant Bah de Poobah for her sixteenth birthday. It took seven months and seven master embroiderers to make it and there is not another like it in the world."

The chamberlain bowed, took the scarf and went and gave it to the hall boy. The hall boy delivered it to the drudge, who showed it to the girl in the room at the back of the kitchen.

"See if you can make one of these!" said the drudge. "It's the queen's own scarf, so it better be good!" Then she snatched the scarf away and rushed out with it, banging the door closed behind her. She handed the scarf back to the hall boy, who passed it on to the chamberlain, who returned it to the dresser to be returned to the cupboard.

The girl sat down and looked at her spinning wheel. There was no hope of her ever being able to make a fancy scarf like that. She gave the wheel a spin, but ended up cracking a finger in the spokes. *What a fool I am!* she thought. *I can't make anything!* With no plan and no hope, she lay down on her little bed and soon fell asleep.

Around midnight she awoke from a terrible dream and couldn't get back to sleep. She kept wondering what to do about the scarf. *Well, I'm awake now,* she thought. *If sneaking worked once, perhaps it will work again.*

She climbed out of bed and carefully opened the door, checking to see if anyone was about. Then she crept from doorway to doorway and hall to hall until, on the far side of the castle, she came to the queen's bedchamber. She carefully opened the door and squeezed inside. Ever so quietly, she searched the room high and low until she came to the cupboard where the dresser kept the queen's clothes. But when she opened it, the door made a little squeak, which woke the queen.

"Who is there?" the queen asked.

The girl didn't know what to do, so she said, "No one at all. It's only the dream of a dream, Your Majesty. Go back to sleep." She stayed very still, and when she made no further noise, the queen drifted off to sleep. The girl found the scarf in the cupboard and took it back to her room.

In the morning, the drudge arrived with a bit of breakfast for the girl and saw the scarf on the bed beside her. "What is this?" she exclaimed. "I can't believe it!" Grabbing the scarf, she rushed off to find the hall boy so it could be shown to the queen.

The queen was in the library, having an important meeting over breakfast with three court judges and two philosophers with long beards. Once again, there was a great kerfuffle outside in the hall. The servants had all followed the chamberlain to the library, wanting to catch a glimpse of the wonderful scarf the girl had made.

Angry at the disturbance, the queen called the chamberlain in. "What's all this ruckus now?" After she'd seen the scarf, she said, "It is nicely done. But it is only a scarf, after all. And isn't the girl lower than a drudge? Give her something more challenging to do. And if you can't get the servants to quiet down, I'll find someone who can. I'll never get to the seaside if I don't finish this."

So the chamberlain went away, thinking, *Find someone else? What did the queen mean? Is she going to take away my job?* Now worried and annoyed, thinking this was a huge waste of everyone's time, he went back to the queen's dresser. Surely she could give him something even more difficult to make that would put a stop to all of this.

The royal dresser was shocked and amazed by the scarf the girl had made. "It's just too bad that it's made by someone lower than a drudge," she said. And she threw the scarf into the back closet so it wouldn't be mixed up with the queen's regular things. Then she went to the queen's wardrobe and brought out a shimmering golden nightgown. "This nightgown was acquired from the great merchant Bah de Poobah for the queen's twenty-first birthday. The girl can't possibly find this much gold thread in one night. Feel how light it is? Each strand is as fine as a spider's web. It was made by the slaves of the Sultan of Sumbaboo. It took them forty weeks to spin the thread and another forty to weave it into fabric."

Promising to return the nightgown immediately, the chamberlain left and found the hall boy, who gave the nightgown to the drudge. The drudge gave the girl only one quick look at it and said she was expected to make a nightgown just the same by the next day.

The girl thought this was all getting to be a bit much. All she wanted was for somebody to show her how to do something useful and she would gladly do it! Yet again, at midnight, she found herself creeping from her room and through the halls to the queen's bedchamber. When she was inside, she looked everywhere for the golden nightgown and found it at last in the wardrobe. But when she opened the door of it, it made a quiet little creak.

"Who is there?" asked the queen.

"No one at all," said the girl. "It's only the dream of a dream, Your Majesty. Go back to sleep."

When the queen drifted off to sleep again, she took the golden nightgown from the wardrobe and brought it back to her room.

In the morning, the drudge arrived with breakfast for the girl and saw the nightgown laid out on the bed beside her. "What is this?" she exclaimed. "I can't believe it!" And scooping up the nightgown, she rushed off to find the hall boy so it could be shown to the queen.

After the hallboy gave it to the chamberlain, half the castle's servants followed him to the library. The chamberlain tried his best to shush them, but they were so loud and there were so many, they couldn't help but make a huge racket.

The queen was at work in the library surrounded by dozens of large, open books. Her hands and lips were stained with ink and she was quite deep in thought when she heard the big excitement out in the hall. "I do wish you would stop bothering me," said the queen, when the chamberlain entered.

The chamberlain took a deep breath and tried to remain calm as he presented the golden nightgown.

"It is extremely nice," said the queen. "But it is only a nightgown, after all. This is the last time I want to hear about any of this. Give the girl something more challenging to do. And if you don't quiet the servants, you'll soon find yourself emptying chamber pots. Now hurry up. I'll never get to the seaside if I don't finish this."

Well, this time the chamberlain had had quite enough. He was determined to solve this ridiculous problem with the drudge's girl. There would be no emptying chamber pots for him! Surely he could get something from the queen's dresser that would be so difficult to make, it would stop all this nonsense in its tracks. Maybe the royal sceptre; maybe the queen's own crown…

But when he knocked on the door of the queen's bedchamber and the dresser opened it, he was in for a surprise. "You'll not get another thing from this room," the dresser said angrily.

The chamberlain was taken aback. "Pardon me?"

"The queen's crane scarf and her golden nightgown have both gone missing. You'll not get another item until they are returned."

"But I did return them," said the chamberlain. "After the girl was shown them, you took them from my own two hands and put them away."

"And now they are gone," the dresser replied. "Find them, or you'll have nothing else." And she grabbed the golden nightgown the girl had made and threw it in the back closet.

The chamberlain went away confused and more than a little annoyed. Whatever was going on here, that girl who was lower than a drudge was making a complete fool out of him, not just in front of the servants, but before the queen herself. How could he put a stop to it, once and for all? He spent the rest of the day pondering the problem and was so distracted he forgot most of his regular duties. When he went to bed that night, he still did not have an answer. What could he get her to make that would be so difficult, so challenging, it would stop all this foolishness forever?

At seven the next morning, after a restless sleep, his eyes suddenly snapped open. "That's it!" he declared. And he dressed quickly and hurried out to find the hall boy. "Bring me to the drudge!" he told him.

Wondering what was going on, the hall boy brought the chamberlain to the drudge, who was already busy at work, chipping dried drips from the underside of a kitchen bench. "Bring me to this girl who makes things!" he demanded.

The drudge was shocked, as was everyone else, to see the chamberlain in so lowly a part of the castle. But she jumped up and led him to the girl's small room in the very back of the kitchen. When she opened the door, the girl squinted up into the open doorway. "Come with me!" the chamberlain ordered.

The girl had never seen this man before. "Who are you," she asked, "and why should I go with you?"

The chamberlain was already angry, but this made him furious. "I am the queen's own chamberlain," he said. "And you are even lower than a drudge! You, in your filthy little room! You will come with me now, as there is something I would like you to make."

The girl thought this strange man was very rude, but she had no choice but to follow him. He led her out of the kitchen and up the stairs to where the morning sun poured in the windows. They went down one hall after another until they entered the main part of the castle. The girl was embarrassed to be seen in her simple dress, for here, even the servants wore crisp uniforms with high boots and collars.

Now, the queen always rose early and was dressed and at work long before her breakfast egg was cooked. She sat at her desk in the library surrounded by stacks of important papers. The chamberlain brought the girl to the door of the library and told her to look in through the keyhole. "Can you make that?" he asked her.

The girl peered through the keyhole at the queen working at her desk. Her gown was pure white and covered in rich gold needlework with diamonds sewn in here and there. The girl looked up to the chamberlain, a little afraid. "I think so," she said. "It's such a beautiful dress."

The chamberlain frowned down at her. "Not the dress, girl. The queen. Can you make another one of her?"

The girl's breath stopped in her throat for a moment and a cold shiver went down her spine. She straightened and faced the chamberlain. "The queen? You want me to make another queen?"

His deep frown lines became even deeper. "That is what I said. You've had your one look. Can you do it?"

The girl gave a little snort of a laugh. She hadn't actually made the pot holder or the scarf or the nightgown. Why would this be any different? "I suppose I can try," she said.

The chamberlain took her by the arm and marched her back to her little kitchen room. By the time they got there, a small crowd of servants and kitchen staff were gathered to see what was going on. He pushed the girl into her room and stood menacingly in the doorway. "Just so you know," he said, "I believe you have been tricking us all. But I don't know how you are doing it. I spoke to the royal dresser this morning. The queen's crane scarf and golden nightgown are both missing from her room. Perhaps the dresser stole them or the queen herself mislaid them. But I think something else happened to the queen's things. You have until the morning to prove your skill and your innocence. Either make another queen, exactly the same in every way, or you will be thrown into the dungeon with the skeletons and left to starve in the dark. You have until morning." And he banged the door closed and left her there alone.

All the servants and kitchen staff watched him leave with wide eyes. The moment he was out of sight, they started talking.

"Did you hear what he said? She has to make another queen."

"That's impossible."

"Oh, that poor girl."

"Yes, but if she does it, that will be something."

It was a long time before the girl stopped staring at the closed door, fearing for her life. She could hear the servants muttering and laughing outside. What had she done? It had all been a game up to this point. But now her life lay in her own two hands, which really did not know how to make anything, let alone a queen. She threw herself on her straw bed and pulled her blanket up over her head.

She slept most of the day and evening away and in the small hours of the morning, she found herself wide awake. *I need to be brave,* she thought, *or there will be no hope at all.* So she went and sat at her spinning wheel. She gave the wheel a turn and once more cracked her finger in the spokes. Painful as it was, she burst out laughing. *How can I make a queen out of straw? I can't even make this wheel turn without hurting myself.* And the more she thought about it, the more she laughed.

Finally she got up and went to sit on her bed and try to be serious. *Well,* she thought at last, *if everything else was done by sneaking, perhaps this can be done, too.*

She stood and crept from her room. When she saw that no one was about, she made her way to the queen's bedchamber and looked everywhere for the scarf and the nightgown. But she couldn't find them. The only place she hadn't looked was the back closet. But when she opened the door, it gave a creak that was even louder than the cupboard or the wardrobe and it woke the queen.

"Who is there?"

"No one at all," said the girl. "It's only the dream of a dream, Your Majesty. Go back to sleep."

It took a long while for the queen to drift off to sleep again. But when she did, the girl tiptoed out to the hallway. There, she pulled the nightgown on over her head and swung the scarf around her neck. Then she pretended to walk gracefully like a queen, with the long nightgown trailing behind her. She didn't really like the smell of the queen's clothes—it was much too flowery for her—but she liked posing this way and that when she came across a mirror. She strode past the windows of the throne room and the library until she saw servants down in the courtyard and guards at the front gate looking up at her in the moonlight.

Finally she crept back into the queen's bedchamber and returned the scarf and nightgown to the back closet.

Then she returned to her room and fell asleep on her little bed.

In the morning, as soon as the chamberlain was awake and dressed, he hurried down to the kitchen to see the girl. Several of the servants and kitchen staff hurried over to hear what the chamberlain had to say. As he expected, there was no second queen in the room. The girl was sitting on her bed with her hands folded. "So?" the chamberlain demanded. "I see you have failed."

The girl gave him a small smile. "How have I failed?" she asked.

"Well, where is the other queen you made?" the chamberlain demanded.

"She left," answered the girl. And as the chamberlain's face began to redden with anger, she added, "You asked me to make her exactly the same and I have done so. She didn't want to stay in such a filthy little room. So she has gone."

"Gone where?" the chamberlain cried.

"Wherever she wishes," said the girl.

"But…did she say anything?"

"A queen," said the girl, calmly, "would never speak to a person such as me. I am lower than a drudge, after all."

Behind him, the servants and kitchen staff all began snickering. The chamberlain whirled and silenced them with, "How dare you! It's all lies. No one has seen this other queen."

The kitchen staff all began talking at once.

"That's not true. The guards caught sight of her in the library window."

"And I saw her in the great hall, walking about."

"The parlour maid saw her too!"

The chamberlain waved them away. "Impossible. Did anyone actually see her here in the girl's room last night?"

"No," answered the cook. "But we could hear the girl working at her spinning wheel and laughing."

The chamberlain was now completely red in the face. "Enough of this!" he said to them all. "I'll hear no more about it. Give this girl something to do that does not involve making things." And he stormed away, determined to forget all this foolishness had ever happened. It was simply not worth his time.

Later that morning, the girl was given actual work as the drudge's helper. It was now her job to scrub the worst of the burnt pots, which were flung into her little room unexpectedly, at all hours of the day. She was glad of this simple job, for it meant she might be able to stay, and she was happy to earn her keep.

While the chamberlain forgot all about the other queen, he was the only one who did. For when a rumour starts in a busy place like a royal castle, it spreads like a grass fire and is very difficult to stamp out. From then on, every time someone heard a mouse in the night, they joked that it was probably the other queen. And whenever the kitchen boy poked his thumb into a butter pot or a bowl of figgy pudding went missing, the other queen was the first one blamed.

After a while, if you asked any of the servants about the other queen, they could have told you quite a story. She only comes out at night and dresses in a shimmering golden nightgown. When it's cold she wears a crane scarf so she doesn't catch a chill. She lets the servants drink beer and ale whenever they want and doesn't mind when the singing gets too loud at the back of the kitchen. She's not like the real queen at all, for she never works hard and lolls about eating figgy pudding all day.

It took some time for the real queen to hear about these rumours, but eventually, hear about them she did. She called the chamberlain into the library one day and demanded an explanation.

"But it's all lies, Your Majesty," the chamberlain told her. "Yes, I asked the girl to make another queen. But no one would ever believe she actually did it."

"Well," the queen answered, "apparently the servants all do. Here." She handed him a scroll of paper. "These are the new rules. No singing or dancing in the kitchen. No eating fat or pudding and certainly no drinking ale or beer. And if anyone is caught stealing food they shall be sent out the front gates after a good thrashing and never work for me again."

The chamberlain had the new rules posted and everyone in the kitchen gathered around to grumble over them.

Eventually, the girl in the back room heard all about it and was sure the kitchen staff blamed her for everything, because now, when the drudge threw pots in for her to scrub, they were pitched in with such violence that they banged off the back wall.

The new rules stopped the rumours and the theft for a little while. But after two weeks, it was even worse than before. During an important meeting in the castle library, it was pointed out that one of the queen's ministers had left greasy fingerprints all over a royal document. "Ha!" he laughed. "I'm so sorry. A little fat got on the book. It must have been that other queen!" The mayors and magistrates all howled with laughter—while the queen sat stiff as stone, turning six shades of red.

The next day, she wrote up another set of rules and the chamberlain did his best to enforce them. But no one seemed to listen. "I'm so sorry, Your Majesty," said the chamberlain. "I've posted the new rules all around the castle. People are now rolling their eyes and saying the wrong queen made them up as a joke!" The queen simply dismissed him, hating that she was too busy to deal with it right then.

A few evenings later, the queen sat at her dressing table, wondering how she could put a stop to all this. "They are drinking beer and dancing down in the kitchen again," she told her dresser. It wasn't often she confided in the old woman, but the queen knew she could always trust her for an honest reaction. "And today, during a meeting, I caught one of my advisors looking at me strangely. I found out later that he was staring at me, wondering if I was the real queen."

"Oh dear," said the dresser.

"Why do they hate me?" the queen blurted.

"They don't hate you, Your Majesty," the dresser said. "They just don't know you. To them, you're all biscuit and no jam."

The queen scowled into her mirror for a moment as the dresser removed her wig. "Your Majesty," the dresser continued, "look what happens when they try to have a little fun. The chamberlain comes out and yells at them. And the kitchen walls are full of new rules. You never have balls or parties or music concerts. You're too busy working!"

The queen suddenly stood. "I can fix this. All I have to do is put my mind to it and work a little harder. I know I can fix this."

The next morning she called her chamberlain into the library and told him to arrange a grand ball and invite all the mayors, ministers and magistrates, along with their husbands and wives. She would show them there was only one queen and she wasn't boring at all.

On the day of the grand ball, the guests arrived expecting to have a wonderful time, since the queen had never had a ball before. Sadly, the queen wanted to set an example and could not put her rules aside. Fancy food and drinks were served, but since she didn't want her servants near butter, beer or sweets, the food was bland and hardly anyone went near the punch bowl. As for music, well, that at least was good. But since the queen was so out of practice at dancing, she didn't want to embarrass herself. So no one else danced, either. They all stood around, nodding and smiling, waiting for the grand ball to be over so they could go home.

In the end, the queen thought the festivities went quite well. Unfortunately, just as everyone was leaving, she overheard a comment from the wife of one of her ministers. "Oh, dear," said the woman, "they should have got the other queen to put on that ball. I've never had a worse time."

The queen was crushed by the comment. She returned to her room and sat on the edge of her bed and stared down at her hands, which were still a little ink-stained. She began twisting at her fingers, trying to rub the ink off. And as she rubbed, more and more desperately, the angrier she became. *If they don't appreciate my hard work,* she thought, *why am I doing it for them? To be treated rudely and made a fool of?*

The following morning, the chamberlain found the queen in the library. It was the first time in years that he had seen her without her high white wig. She was dressed in a hat and long travelling coat and there were three large bags at her feet. "Are you going on a trip, Your Majesty?" he asked.

"Yes," she barked back at him. "And I will not be doing any work while I am gone. Here," she said, heaping a pile of letters and papers into his arms. "I need you to finish this. And this, too!" she said, adding more. "I am going to the seaside."

The chamberlain had to blink his eyes a few times to make sense of it all. "But...but for how long? Will you be back before your birthday? It's only a few weeks away."

"Don't bother me with details," the queen snapped back. "I expect so. But I'll send for a carriage when I'm ready. One more thing," she said. "You will clear up this problem of the other queen. Do you understand?"

The chamberlain gave a little bow. "As you wish, Your Majesty."

The queen swept out of the room and as soon as the footman had loaded her bags into the royal carriage, she was away.

The chamberlain stood at the door for the longest while, scratching his head. What had just happened? After all her talk, the queen was actually going to the seaside! As happy as he was for her, he suddenly realized how much work he had before him. On top of his regular duties, he now had all the queen's work, too. Where was he going to find time to deal with this business of the other queen?

Three days later, the queen arrived at the seaside. It was just as she remembered it—the beautiful sandy beach, the boats bobbing in the bay, and the evening sun rolling off the edge of the sea like a huge pearl. Even the little seaside inn where she had stayed was exactly the same. What she failed to remember was that everything smelled like fish. And she did not like fish very much.

She spent two fitful nights with her nose covered with a scented handkerchief. But it was no good. Beautiful as the place was, she couldn't stand it for another day, let alone for weeks on end. She had to go home, and quickly. The trouble was, her carriage was already far away and even if she sent the swiftest messenger, it wouldn't return for days.

The following morning she was so fed up, she went out and found another way home. There was a man with a simple cart staying at the inn. She discovered he was on his way to a town near her castle to visit his cousin for a few days and she hired him to take her along. Sadly, it rained constantly all the way there. She arrived late at night, soaked to the skin, to find lights still burning in the castle kitchen and fiddle music and singing floating through its windows and doors. The chamberlain had obviously failed, she thought. But she was secretly glad the kitchen staff were still awake, for she was hungry and desperate for something warm to drive the chill from her.

When she reached her room, she found the fire was out and she had nowhere to light a candle. So she changed out of her wet travelling clothes in the dark and was happy to find a nightgown and scarf on the floor of her closet. She put them on, then, hungrier than ever, down she went to the kitchen.

But when she arrived and stood in the archway, she ended up getting more of a shock than the kitchen staff. The music stopped, the drinking stopped and all eyes turned to the woman in the archway.

"Oh!" exclaimed the cook. "It's the other queen!"

The queen began looking around. Then she looked down and saw she was wearing the golden nightgown and the crane scarf and realized they meant her. "I—I—" she stammered. "I've just come for something to eat and drink."

Everyone was deathly silent for a moment. Then the cook said, "Some figgy pudding, perhaps?" A few servants chuckled.

The queen suddenly realized she had a perfect opportunity here. Her rules had failed. The chamberlain had obviously failed. But if the servants wouldn't listen to the real queen, who was strict and boring, perhaps they would listen to the other queen, who liked to have fun and was not boring at all. "Absolutely," said the queen. "Bring me some figgy pudding."

The servants' eyes went wide and they ran off to the pantry, waking anyone who was still asleep, saying the other queen was out and about. They hurried back with the figgy pudding and watched wide-eyed as the queen sat up on the big table in the middle of the kitchen and ate a bite. Then when she asked for hot tea to warm herself up, they got it for her so quickly, she thought there would be an accident.

The queen was quite nervous with everyone staring at her. She wasn't sure how the other queen was supposed to behave. But she'd better think of something fun, and quickly, she thought, or the servants might suspect she was the real queen, just dressed up. "Bring me a pot of butter!" she ordered. When they brought it, she stuck her thumb in, and licked it clean.

The eyes of all the servants around her were big as saucers. She lost count of how many times she heard someone whisper, "I told you she was real." And soon someone brought out a fiddle again, and they all began to sing and dance around.

While everyone was making merry, the queen noticed a not-very-big girl in an old dress staring at her from beside the fireplace. She seemed very interested in the queen's odd behaviour. Was this the girl who had made the scarf and golden nightgown? The girl was the only person in the kitchen who was eyeing her suspiciously. Fearing the girl would expose her secret, the queen asked the cook who the girl was, and sure enough, it was *that* girl.

"Oh, the poor thing," said the queen. "I owe her so much, and she seems to have so little. Make sure she has a nice new dress by morning."

"Yes, Your Majesty."

The queen couldn't stand the girl staring at her like that, spoiling all her fun. So she ordered everyone to bed and whisked herself away down the halls and back to her room. There, she lay in bed, excited, embarrassed, and afraid that the girl might expose her, all in a confused jumble. *Tomorrow,* she thought, *tomorrow I will get them all to stop lying and stealing and blaming the other queen.*

The next morning, the drudge brought the girl a fine new dress. "It seems you're the other queen's favourite. Ha!" And she flung the dress into the room.

The girl changed into it and sat down on her bed to admire the color and the fabric, which was by far the nicest dress she had ever worn. *This is so beautiful,* she thought. *I wish I knew how to sew like this.*

The queen stayed in her bedchamber the entire day, letting only her dresser know that she had returned from the seaside. For some reason, she had no desire to go down to the library to work. Instead, she slept in late and lolled about in her bed till mid-afternoon. She was confident that tonight, she would dispel all the nasty rumours of the other queen and things would return to normal.

But that night, when she put on the golden nightgown and the crane scarf and went down to the kitchen for her figgy pudding, she was no further ahead. After her pudding, she had a little beer, which tasted very good. So had another little beer and that made her get up and dance a very stiff and dizzy jig. With the servants all jolly and toasting her good health, she realized her plan was working, even though that girl kept peering around the fireplace at her again. The only thing worse than the problem of this other queen, she thought, was the threat of being found out that she was dressing up as her.

"From now on," she told the cook, worried that the girl would tell her secret, "give that poor thing the same dinner you serve the queen. She looks so thin."

"Yes, Your Majesty."

Once again she hurried back to her room, a mess of mostly happy emotions and wondering how she could ever have danced a jig with the stable boy.

The next day the drudge elbowed open the door of the girl's room. "There you go, Miss Favourite," she said. And she flung a slab of beef at her with a great, "Ha!" and stormed back down the hall.

The girl ate the beef, which was covered in deep brown gravy, thinking, *Oh, the cook is so lucky to know how to make such delicious things.*

That night, the queen was determined to hold fast to her plan and stop all this nonsense about the other queen entirely. She put on the golden nightgown, swung the crane scarf around her neck, and down to the kitchen she went. But one bite of figgy pudding and she was lost. They let her have some beer and brought all the butter pots, one after another, for her to stick her thumbs in.

Trying to ignore the girl by the fireplace, she danced till her feet were sore and her stomach ached with laughter. But still the girl continued to stare, the only person who knew for sure that she was just the real queen dressed up. What a fix she would be in if the girl told everyone the truth!

"That poor girl is there again," she told the cook. "You must speak to the hall boy and have him find her a room near the front of the castle. She needs a big bed and warm blankets if she's ever to grow up strong and happy."

"Yes, Your Majesty."

The queen was so tipsy by then, she could barely walk. Muttering to herself about how much she hated wearing a wig and working so hard every day, she staggered back to her room, with butter up to her eyebrows and pudding in her hair.

The next day, the hallboy fetched the girl to bring her to a fine room at the front of the castle. As they passed the other servants in their crisp uniforms, she was glad to be seen in her new dress, as long as she hid the beef stain on the front of it. When they arrived, she sat on the big comfortable bed, trying to figure out how they wove the sheets so wonderfully smooth. *Whoever made this,* she thought, *is the luckiest person in the world.*

Now, the queen's birthday was fast approaching. The chamberlain, who had to organize the celebration for it, was already overwhelmed by the queen's regular duties.

He sat in the royal library with papers piled all around him, going over a checklist for the party. Decorations were being installed. Invitations had gone out. Bah de Poobah himself was delivering a fabulous dress that had been ordered as a gift for the queen. Was there anything he was forgetting?

The moment the chamberlain had this thought, he remembered something very important. The queen had asked him to take care of that other queen before she returned from the seaside. As panic set in, he stood up and took a few deep, worried breaths. "How can I solve a problem like that?" he lamented, just as a servant entered the library with his tea. "The other queen is just a rumour! A pack of lies!"

The servant looked for a place to set down the tea tray. "Pardon me, sir. But the other queen is not just a rumour. Every night I see her down in the castle kitchen."

"What?" exclaimed the chamberlain. "What are you saying?"

The servant told the chamberlain all about how the other queen had been dancing around the kitchen, drinking beer and eating figgy pudding.

"Oh, thank you," said the chamberlain. "I'm so glad I can fix this so easily. You've saved me so much trouble." And right then, he called the guards from the hallway and told them to go down to the kitchen that night and capture the other queen.

"And what shall we do with her then?" asked one of the guards.

"Take her out to the woods and hang her from a high tree. That will be quick. And you may as well take the girl who made the other queen, too. We don't want her making another one."

So that night, after another giddy time in the castle kitchen, the tipsy, butter-stained queen returned to her room and slipped into bed. But just as she was falling asleep, the guards came in and grabbed her. They grabbed the girl from her new, fancy bedroom, too. Both were rolled in a carpet and carried out into the dark to be pitched onto a crude wagon. Then off to the woods the wagon went.

Unlike the queen, the girl was used to sneaking out of tight places. Not knowing why she and the queen had been grabbed, she popped her head out early on and listened to the guards talking to one another. When she heard that the guards were going to hang them from a high tree in the woods, she was determined to get away. She waited until the trees of the wood blocked the light from the moon and stars then, while the queen stayed suffocating in the rolled-up carpet, groaning about the smell of dust and feet, the girl wriggled her way out and jumped to the ground.

She waited till the wagon was out of sight, then hurried back to the edge of the woods. *Now what am I going to do?* she wondered. And she ran across farmers' fields and squirmed under hedges like a rabbit, knowing she could never go back to the castle.

Deep in the woods, the guards stopped the wagon and lifted down the carpet. They knew right away that the girl was missing and far from being annoyed, the guards were relieved. Gently, they spilled the queen out on the ground.

"Our deepest apologies, Your Majesty," the first guard said with a bow. "But the chamberlain ordered us to take you away and hang you from a high tree in the woods. That, we cannot do. Your only crime is making merry, and no one, queen or pauper, should die for that."

"You shall be richly rewarded," said the queen, glad to be alive. She knew it was her own order to the chamberlain that had gotten her into this fix. But she needed some time to figure out what to do next. "Return to the castle," she told the guards. "Tell the chamberlain you have done what he has asked and I am now dead."

The guards did not like leaving the queen there to fend for herself, but they bowed and off they went. When they arrived at the castle they told the chamberlain that they'd taken the queen and the girl out to the woods and done his bidding, hanging them both from a high tree. The chamberlain sighed in relief. "Thank goodness. That's one more task off my desk."

Shivering in the night, the queen left the woods and began walking back to the castle. She spent the next hour wishing poxes and boils on the chamberlain and making noises like "Pffft!" and "Uggh!" as she walked along in the moonlight. Her plan was to return to the castle and pretend she was just getting back from the seaside. Nothing could be simpler, she thought, though she deeply regretted that the other queen would stay dead. There would be no more figgy pudding, no more beer or dancing when the real queen returned. And the thought of those endless meetings, those piles of papers and everyone thinking she was stiff and boring almost made her turn around and go back to the woods. One thing changed her mind.

She had walked on through the night until she came to the high road. The sun was only beginning to rise and the travellers on the road were few. When she saw anyone coming, she ducked into the bushes beside the road until they passed. But one man driving a simple cart made the queen stop in her tracks to wait for him.

"I know that man," she said to herself, for it was the carter who had brought her back to the castle from the seaside. She strode forward and stopped him on the road. "Do you recognize me?"

The man immediately jumped down from his cart and bowed deeply. "Of course, Your Majesty. But what on earth has happened to you? I delivered you quite safely to your castle not seven days ago."

"Never mind about that," the queen said. "I need your help and will pay you richly for it."

"Of course, Your Majesty. Anything you wish."

The queen explained clearly what she wanted and the carter bowed and helped her up onto his cart. Then he turned the cart around and they bumped along toward the castle throughout the day. When they arrived late that evening, the queen asked to be let off at the kitchen door. "You know what to do," she said to the carter.

"Indeed, Your Majesty." With a tip of his hat, he went around to the front of the castle, and asked the guards at the gate if he might speak to the chamberlain.

"He is much too busy to speak to you," one of them replied. "What is it you want?"

"Well," said the carter, "I brought the queen back from the seaside about a week ago and I still haven't been paid."

"As far as we know," the guard said, "the queen has not returned."

"Oh, but she has. I dropped her off here myself."

One of the guards went into the castle and began making inquiries. Not one of the servants he spoke to had seen the queen. That is, until he asked the queen's dresser.

"Why yes," said the dresser. "She has been back for a week. I'm just putting her bags away now. She has been hiding in her room and doesn't want to speak to anyone. You had better pay the carter."

So the guard went to see the chamberlain to get the money to pay the carter.

"What is it?" the chamberlain barked when the guard entered the library, for even though the hour was quite late, the chamberlain was still hard at work.

The guard told him a carter was at the gate to collect his fee for bringing the queen back to the castle from the seaside. "I didn't believe it," said the guard, "but I've just come from the royal dresser. And it's true. The queen has been back for nearly a week. Apparently she's been hiding in her room. I saw the three bags she took to the seaside sitting on the floor."

All the color drained out of the chamberlain's face. *I've killed the wrong queen,* he thought as the important papers he'd been working on dropped from his hands.

Seeing the chamberlain's distress, the guard asked, "Are you all right, sir?"

"I…I'm fine," he stammered. With shaking hands he brought a small money box out from under the desk. "Here." He handed the guard a fistful of coins. "Take this for the carter. Not a word of this to anyone, do you hear?"

"Of course, sir," the guard said with a bow, and out he went to pay the carter.

As soon as the guard was gone, the chamberlain leaped up and began pacing the room, trampling the papers he had dropped on the floor. "This is the end of me. I've killed the wrong queen," he muttered. "I've killed the wrong queen!"

Looking as pale as a dead man himself, he made his way out of the library, his chin quivering with fear, his chest tight with agonies of remorse. He rushed to his room and began packing a bag, intending to flee the castle before news got out and he was captured and hung for murdering the queen.

Knowing the guards were by the front door, he thought he'd go out the back way. But he was no more than ten steps down the stairs when he heard the sound of fiddle music coming from the kitchen. Creeping to the bottom of the stairs, he hid himself behind the archway to the kitchen and peered into the room. Just as he feared, there was the other queen, a glass of ale in her hand, smacking her lips with a mouthful of figgy pudding.

His first thought was, *Oh! This proves I've killed the wrong one.* His second thought was, *My goodness, does she ever look like the real queen!* Right then, he had the glimmer of an idea. He might not have to leave the castle after all.

Hiding his bag in a dark corner, he strode into the kitchen. Immediately, the music and merriment stopped.

The other queen had just stuck her thumb into a pot of butter and looked up, mildly shocked that she had been discovered. "Yes?" she asked. "May I help you?"

"Yes, Your Majesty," said the chamberlain with a small bow. "You certainly may. Might I speak with you privately for a moment?"

He brought her around to the back of the kitchen, and by chance, into the little room where the sneaking girl had stayed. "Your Majesty, I have done a terrible thing. By mistake, I have sent the real queen to her death. She has been hung from a high tree in the woods and is now dead. Your appearance is exactly the same as the real queen. I am a desperate man who needs to hide his crime. I will do anything you ask. I am hoping you will consent to play the real queen during the day."

The queen raised an eyebrow and licked a bit of the butter from her thumb. "I don't know," she said. "I think it would be a lot of work."

"Oh no, Your Majesty," blurted the chamberlain. "I can take care of the meetings and paperwork and all the queen's regular duties. And you can certainly continue to visit the kitchen in the evenings. Please, please, will you help me?"

As the chamberlain spoke, a very small smile appeared on the queen's lips. The longer the chamberlain spoke, the larger the smile became. Finally, she sucked the last of the butter from her thumb with a smack and said, "I believe I will."

So the queen's birthday was held a few days later, and all the important people came to wish her well. Bah de Poobah himself arrived in a fancy carriage pulled by four sorrel mares. He was a very large, exotic-looking man. The toes of his shoes curled up and around, as did his thick moustaches and for that matter, his eyebrows. On his head was a silk turban with a fan of peacock feathers sticking up in the front. He presented the queen with her birthday gift with incredible pomp and ceremony.

It was the most beautiful dress that anyone had every laid eyes on, covered in fine embroidery and glimmering jewels. "These are the rarest of gems," said Bah de Poobah in a deep, resonant voice. "It took seven years for the slaves of the Sultan of Sumbaboo to mine them. The silken thread is from the blind spiders in the depths of a cavern under the Seventh Sea. It took twelve master embroiderers twelve months to create the intricate needlework, so that Her Majesty might have this beautiful gift on her birthday."

The queen, who seemed relaxed and happy, accepted the gift and made sure the merchant was filled to his round cheeks with fine food and excellent drink.

Unlike every other festive event that had been held in the castle over the years, there was lively music and wine and good ale served by the barrel. The queen danced every dance and even fell down on the floor from laughing so hard.

"What an extraordinary change in the queen," the guests noted. "Her trip to the seaside seems to have done wonders for her. This is the best party I have ever been to. We shall surely accept every invitation from now on."

In the days following, the queen's mood continued to improve. All the rules posted in the kitchen were taken down. In their place, the queen gave the servants a large pot of butter every Friday. They were told if they kept their music and dancing for that one day of the week, they could have a keg of ale to go with it. And no one seemed to mind that at all.

The queen continued to hold fancy dress balls and soon met a handsome gentleman who, it turned out, kept her far busier and happier than work ever had.

Her chamberlain did his best to keep his word, but it became increasingly difficult. He was frequently found in the library, crying over the stacks of papers on his desk. Toward the end of the second month, he collapsed from exhaustion and was forced to retire. The queen hired seven people to replace him and even they were kept busy from morning till night.

As for the girl, she walked all through that first night and well into the next day. She drank cold water from a little stream but had nothing to eat at all, and soon her stomach was grumbling. With nowhere else to go, she went in the direction of the little village where the old woman lived, selling her ugly cups. *I need to eat,* she thought, *but I don't want to be thrown out into the street like dishwater if I make one little mistake.* Still, her legs took her to the village and right up to the old woman's house.

But when she got to the window where the old woman sat, all she got was, "Ha! You again! You had your chance, so goodbye."

The girl walked a few steps away, but the pain in her stomach made her stop on the road. "Please," she said, turning around. "I will do everything just as you say."

The old woman replied, "And what makes you think I care about you? Isn't there somewhere else you'd like to be? Go on, get out of here. I have no reason to believe you."

The girl turned and walked to the edge of the village, her chin trembling with fear and frustration, not knowing where to go. Her mother was gone, her sisters were dead. Even their little house had sunk into the bog. *Maybe I'll die like them,* she thought.

She took a few deep breaths and a moment later found herself stamping her foot in the dust. *Enough of this!* she thought. And she turned around and went back to the old woman at the window.

"Please," she said. "I will sit selling your cups for the first year. I will knead the clay for the second and watch you carefully for the third. And I promise, I will never look behind the curtain."

The old woman saw the girl's little chin wobbling and took pity on her. "Fine," she said. "You do that and we'll get along well."

The old woman told her again, with a jab of her bony finger, never to pass the curtain. "Or you'll land in the street like a pan of dishwater."

"What if you're dying and need my help?"

"Then let me die or out you can go to starve, for all I care."

So the girl was let into the house and began her work that very day, sitting at the window selling the woman's incredibly ugly cups. She was given a piece of bread and a bite of fish every day at noon and slept on the hearth with her two arms for a pillow.

The old woman was a terrible cup maker. What was worse, she would only make one or two cups at a time. The rest of the day she spent down in her cellar—digging clay for the cups, the girl imagined. Once a week, the old woman would leave the house with a bundle under her arm and return with a loaf of bread and a fish for them to eat.

The girl sat at the window every day the whole of the following year. Hardly anyone stopped to buy up a cup. They would take one look, see how ugly they were, and keep walking. But the girl kept her word and stayed put.

The next year the old woman brought lumps of cold, wet clay from behind the curtain every day and made her squeeze and knead them until her hands were numb. When the lumps were warm and supple enough, the woman would take them away and bring her more to work at while she sat at the window.

The year after that, true to her word, the old woman brought her potter's wheel out and for an hour every day, the girl watched her at work. It was boring beyond anything she had ever done, but she paid close attention and the woman never spoke of throwing her out.

Then one day, just as the old woman came home with their food for the week and went behind the curtain, the girl heard a great bang. The next thing she knew the old woman was calling up to her from the cellar, "Help! Help!"

The girl rose, about to go and help her, but stopped short.

"Help! Help!" the old woman cried. "I've fallen down the stairs and I can't get up!"

"I cannot help you," said the girl. "You said I could never pass the curtain, even if you were dying."

"I am dying! I've broken my old bones and can't get up!"

"Then you shall die," said the girl, rubbing the tears from her eyes. "I can't help you."

The next thing she knew, the old woman was tromping up the stairs and throwing the curtain aside, making the girl jump back. The woman did not seem injured at all. "Good for you, girl. Now I know I can trust you." She held the curtain aside. "Come with me now. There is something I need to show you. It's alright. The test is over. Don't be afraid."

So the girl followed the old woman past the curtain and down into the cellar. There, at the foot of the stairs, was a muddy little room with shelves of cups on either side. As the old woman led her farther into it, though, she was surprised to find that the cellar was much larger than she'd imagined.

The old woman stopped in an area with a beautiful wooden floor and exquisite tapestries hanging on the walls. To one side was a stove and a sitting room with rich carpets and cushions. And in the middle stood a loom for making beautiful cloth and beside it, boxes of ribbon and thread.

"What is all this?" the girl exclaimed.

The old woman shrugged. "I like to make things," she said. "People think I only make cups. But the man I sell my things to pays me to keep my skills a secret. While you sit at the window, I make scarves and dresses and nightgowns. I deliver my goods once a week to the merchant. His name is Bah de Poobah. He tells everyone, 'Oh, it takes forty weeks and forty master weavers to make a scarf.' But the truth is, it usually takes me about a three days to make a nice one. Of course, he's not going to tell his customers that.

"Now," she continued, "I am getting old and I don't want these skills to be lost when I am gone. You have learned patience, sitting at the window. Your hands have grown strong, working the clay, and your eyes keen, watching me at my potter's wheel. You are now ready to learn; if you like, I can show you everything I know."

The girl remembered her mother and her sisters sitting around the fire, with no place for her. "I've always wanted to make things," she said to the old woman. "That would be very nice."

So she worked with the old woman day after day and learned how to sew and weave and embroider. She loved the feel of the silk thread and the satin fabric. But even more, she loved how one little stitch today became a thousand stitches by week's end, and the result was so beautiful she squirmed with excitement as she fell asleep, eager to start work again in the morning.

After a few years, the old woman died. The girl stayed on in the house and continued her wonderful work. Every week, she delivered a bundle to the merchant named Bah de Poobah, who sold her scarves and gowns in the courts of queens around the world. After a few more years, the girl grew into a very contented young woman. She married and had children of her own, who would sit at the window squishing lumps of clay and making ugly cups. She taught them everything she knew and later, did the same for her grandchildren. But unlike her childhood home, which sank deeper into the ground as each person left, she eventually had to put a second story on her house. Everyone wanted to live there. For no matter how much her children loved sneaking more than working, there was always room around the fire.

The Miller

and the Old Hag

The Miller and the Old Hag

There was once a miller and his wife who had three sons. Day after day, the miller tried to get his sons to work in the mill with him. He coaxed and he pleaded, but try as he might, the boys would do nothing to help. So the miller had to do everything himself.

The truth was, the boys were very talented, and slaving over grain and flour all day seemed like torture to them. The youngest of the boys wanted to be a musician, the middle boy a painter, and the eldest dreamed of one day building bridges and palaces.

Their father, too, had once had such dreams. In his younger days, he had wanted to be a sculptor. He had a natural hand for it and a keen eye, and the neighbors all said he would be famous one day. But then he married and soon had children to feed. So he had gritted his teeth and taken over the mill when his own father died, leaving his mallet and chisels on a shelf to gather dust.

One day, the miller decided enough was enough. The boys were now strong young men and were complaining daily that there wasn't enough to eat. If they didn't work, he decided, they wouldn't eat, either. He would sell the ox that turned his millstone, buy a larger stone so he could grind more grain, and get his sons to turn it.

When his boys heard this idea, they were not very pleased with it and loudly said so. Back and forth they fought and argued while their mother crouched at the kitchen fire, asking the supper pot for the strength to keep quiet.

Once they'd eaten and calmed themselves a bit, the boys tried to be reasonable. They presented their own idea of what should be done. "Please, Father," said the eldest son. "Don't buy a new millstone. Use the gold from selling the ox to help us become apprentices in our own trades."

"Who will turn the millstone, then?" said their father. "Me alone?"

The eldest son answered, "I have found a stream deep underground, below the mill house. I know of a way to use the rushing water to turn the millstone for you."

"What a foolish idea!" said the miller. "And what will that teach you and your brothers? Nothing!"

"Father," said the second son, "you have to understand, the three of us could become millers like you, but it would cost us our dreams. Yet we cannot leave, for we have no means to support ourselves."

"Then you must buckle up your boots and accept your fate," said the miller. "I will not change my mind."

Now, the miller's wife thought of her husband as a rather foolish but big-hearted man. When his boys were young, he looked at their little hands and said, "Keep them out of the mill house. I don't want them hurt by the ox or the heavy stone." But now his big-heartedness was getting their family into trouble, for if he'd had helpers all along to increase their business, they wouldn't be in this fix. One of the boys could have coaxed the ox around and around. Another could have been bagging flour and the third, helping customers while their father did the heaviest work. It was only now, when their sons were grown and had minds of their own, that the trouble began.

"You didn't want them in the mill," she told him, "and now you do. You can't expect them to change, just like that!"

The miller shook his head. "They were weak little children then. Now they are supposed to be strong young men. And look what you've done to them! All this music and drawing and everything. You just wish you had a girl!"

And it was true, she realized. Though she and her husband were now too old to have more children, she had always hoped for a daughter. She'd even kept a box of toys and girlish clothes from her childhood up in the rafters of their little house. "Well," she said, "whatever talents our sons have, you know they didn't come from me. I only brought out in them what was already there."

If there was something the miller's wife was good at, it was solving everyone else's troubles. But this time, she could think of no solution. Night after night, she lay awake with their voices ringing in her head. Surely, she thought, there must be way out of this.

The night before her husband was to take the ox to market she had an idea, but it involved enormous sacrifice, and her hopes and fears made that night another sleepless one. While her husband slept, she plucked up her courage, went and woke her sons, and brought them into the mill house and sat them down.

"We are all miserable," she said, "and I can't stand to see any of you unhappy. I have a plan that could send you all off to your own trades. We'll each have to play a part. Two of you will pretend to be thieves, the third will be a beggar and I will disguise myself as an old hag. Now listen carefully."

When she was done, the two youngest boys laughed at the idea, but the eldest shook his head.

"What is it?" asked his mother. "You don't think it will work?"

"That's not it," said the eldest. "If your plan works, we will be the happiest men in the whole country. If it doesn't, we will be no better off than we are today."

"Then what is it?"

"Mother," he said, "You have your dreams, too. Why should we and our father get everything and you nothing? When you were a girl, didn't you want to open a shop to sell fine hats and dresses?"

The mother considered for a moment. "My boys," she said, "That was long before you were born. I have only one dream now. If I can make you and your father content, then I will be content. Don't concern yourselves with me. It is your father you must worry about."

The following morning, the miller led his ox along the high road on the long trip to the village market. It was a hard thing he had to do, he knew. But he couldn't feed his grown sons without a larger millstone. After he sold his ox, though, it was going to be difficult to get his sons to turn it.

There were not many people on the road this early in the day, but the miller kept a sharp eye out for bandits. He passed a beggar with a ragged blanket over his head, limping along slowly with the aid of a crutch. The beggar asked him for a penny, and though the miller had only one penny to his name, he gave it to the man, thinking he would soon have all the gold from selling his ox. A little farther on, he passed an old hag who was sleeping under a tree. Then he saw no one for a long while.

About three miles along, the road passed through a dark wood. A few of his neighbors had been robbed here and the miller tightened his grip on the ox's rope and quickened his pace. But he was only a dozen steps into the wood when two men in masks jumped onto the road in front of him. Though he put up a good fight, he made the mistake of keeping a grip on the rope so he wouldn't lose his ox, and the men quickly overpowered him. They used the rope to tie him to a tree, then hurried away, pulling the ox by its halter.

It took a long time for him to get loose. By then, there was no hope of catching the thieves. What was he to do now? Without the ox to sell, he couldn't afford a new millstone. His sons would have to turn the old one day after day, and after all their work, there wouldn't be any more bread on the table for them than there was right now. What kind of a father was he, that he should treat his boys like this?

Broken in spirit, he started on his way home, only to come upon the beggar skipping down the road toward him. His limp was gone and so was the crutch he had been using.

"I'm healed! I'm healed!" the beggar shouted, skipping past the miller like a child on the first day of spring.

A little closer to home, the miller was stopped by the old hag who had been sleeping under the tree at the side of the road. She was dressed in rags, and her head and face were wrapped in a tattered old scarf. Supporting her bent old back with the beggar's crutch, she was fiddling with a penny between her boney fingers.

"Life is short," she croaked. "Help a poor old woman and she will help you."

"Ha!" the miller snorted. "How could you ever help me?"

"I can solve the troubles of any man or child," said the old hag. She suddenly took hold of him by the collar of his shirt and looked up close into his left eye. "I know just what you need," she said. "Your trade is not your chosen one, but soon that will change." Then she pushed his head over and looked into his right eye. "You think your children are lazy, but soon they will work without you asking." Finally, she looked him squarely in both eyes and said, "You have had something stolen, but soon you will no longer need it." Then she let go of his collar and stepped back. "To have these things, what feeds you must feed me."

The miller stood up and rubbed his neck. He didn't know what to think of the words of this crazy old woman. But he had seen the skipping beggar with his own eyes and was desperate for any help she might be able to give him. "What do I have to do?" he asked her.

"Carry me to where your troubles lie," she said, "and you will see."

So he put the old woman on his back and began walking home. The hag still had the beggar's crutch and when he slowed in the least, she thwacked him on the shins to get him going again.

It took a long time for them to get to the mill house, but when they arrived, he set the woman down. "Now what?" he asked her.

She pointed to the mill house door. "Go in and see."

The miller went to the door, opened it carefully and stepped inside. The first thing he saw was his old millstone standing on end against the wall. And in its place was a large new millstone, ready for work.

"I can't believe it!" he exclaimed. He called for his wife and sons to come but he got no answer. So he rushed out to the old woman and began thanking her for her gift.

She pushed him aside, saying, "Oh, that's only the half of it." She hobbled inside the mill house and began rapping on the new millstone with the beggar's crutch. Then she went to the flour bin, scooped up two handfuls of flour and flung it into the air all around.

When the air cleared and the miller stopped coughing, he heard something he did not expect: the sound of his mill at work. The new millstone seemed to be turning by itself, without ox or man. He looked everywhere for the source, trying to figure out what was making the new millstone turn, but found nothing. In a panic, he turned to the old hag. "What have you done? How is this millstone turning?"

The old woman smiled and walked over to a dusty shelf in the corner of the mill house. There lay the mallet and chisels the miller had set aside as a young man.

"Here," she said, handing him the tools.

"What are these for?"

The old woman squinted up at him and said, "Those are to get your sons out of the stone. You wanted them to turn it. Now they are turning it."

Horrified, the miller stared at the old hag in disbelief.

"If you choose," she said, "you may let them grind your grain forever. That is what you wanted, isn't it? But if you want them back, you must find them in the stone and free them with these tools."

The miller searched for words. "But...how do I bring them to life again?"

The old hag grinned and said, "This gift will last seven years. But to keep our bargain, what feeds you must feed me. You grind farmers' grain and keep some as payment. Take half the flour you earn every month and leave it at the crossroads. After seven years I will return and restore your sons to life, from whatever shape you have carved them."

With that, the old hag left the mill house and hobbled off down the road, leaving the miller staring at the tools in his hands.

He waited and waited for his wife and sons to return. At last, just before dark, his wife arrived home, her coat and hair in disarray.

"Our boys have disappeared!" she exclaimed as soon as she was in the door. "One minute they were here and the next they were gone! I've been searching for them all day!"

Distressed, the miller had no idea what to do. He told her the whole story of the hag and the ox and the millstone.

"You can't blame yourself for what those bandits and that old woman did," she told him. "Just do your best to get our sons back."

The next day, the miller took the new stone from the mill and laid it up on his big workbench. When he put the old grinding stone back on the mill, it didn't turn at all.

"Oh, what have I done?" he lamented.

Over the next several months, when his sons did not return, he came to believe the old hag and left half the grain he earned, by his own and his wife's sweat, at the crossroads. It took a long time for him to gather enough courage to even think about learning to carve. But one day, his wife caught him poking with his knife at chunks of turnip at the supper table. After a while, she saw him outside after a long day's work, whittling twigs or gouging shapes out of small blocks of wood. She would smile to herself but say nothing.

After a year of practicing on wood, he began bringing rocks home from the river and cutting crude faces into them. He had a natural talent for the work, but his heart sank whenever he thought of going near the millstone with a chisel.

Day in and day out, he and his wife took turns pushing the old millstone around and around to grind the grain that farmers brought in. Month in and month out, he had no choice but to leave the old hag half of the flour they earned. His customers began asking about all the carvings he had lying around the yard and soon he had small commissions for stone steps and lintels. By the fourth year, he was asked to carve stone animals for a new fountain in a far city. With the money from that, he found he could spend less time on mill work and more on his carving. But it wasn't until the end of the fourth year that he thought to put a chisel to the stone that stood in his mill house.

Even then he hesitated, and spent three sleepless nights keeping his wife awake with his tossing and turning. Finally, he sat up in bed and told her what was bothering him. "I'm so afraid to start. What if I make a mistake? And after all my trouble, what if they don't look or act like you and me?"

She said nothing for a long while, thinking of the differences between a man's work and her own. "Well," she said at last. "Those boys were made once, and you didn't care for the job I did. Now it's your turn."

The next day the miller walked around the millstone a hundred times without touching it. He had spent many weeks drawing lines in chalk on it where he would begin to cut. But staring at them now, though he could find no fault with them, he kept turning away and turning away. Finally, he worked up his courage and stood to face the millstone.

And he began.

For many a long day and sleepless night, the miller's tears dampened the hard stone. *I have made dozens of beautiful carvings,* he kept thinking, *I should be able to do this.* There were good days, when a leg or an arm would emerge from the millstone. But years had passed since the miller had looked upon the faces of his sons. The work of carving their fair cheeks, their delicate ears and eyes took more pained hours of standing back and trying to recall than time spent removing chips of stone.

At last, the day came when he was done all the carving, the smoothing and the polishing. Three stone figures lay curled in a circle on his workbench. *Perhaps,* he thought, *this is the best work any man has ever done.* When his wife came in to see his accomplishment, they wept in each other's arms for gladness.

Not long after, while the miller's wife was off at the river for water, a knock came at the mill house door. When the miller answered it, there stood the hag he had met on the high road exactly seven years before. She had grown fat on the miller's flour. "Well, miller," she croaked, patting her belly, "it was a fair trade, I must say."

Then she went to the flour bin, gathered two handfuls of flour and began throwing it into the air all around the mill house. When the cloud of dust settled, the stone figures were gone, and in their place were the miller's three sons.

With a wild cackle, the old hag hobbled out the door and down the road, never to be seen again.

The father stood staring at his sons for a long while, his eyes brimming with tears, not knowing what to say. When the boy's mother returned, she found her husband with his arms around his sons, sobbing with happiness, saying, "Oh, I'm such a fool. You are so much better than I'd imagined. Welcome. Welcome home."

So the father became a sculptor and earned a far better wage than any miller. Though he told the story a thousand times to neighbors and customers and anyone else who would listen, his wife never told him what really happened: how gold from the ox had bought the millstone he had carved and how the flour he left at the crossroads had paid for his sons' apprenticeships. The youngest son had become a fine musician, the second son a skilled painter and the eldest was now a master builder.

"You can thank that old hag," said the miller to his sons. "She must have given you those skills."

"There is no question of that," said the eldest. "But I think your hard work had something to do with it."

The eldest son never forgot about his mother's dream and her long sacrifice. He spoke to his father and his brothers and each saved a little bit of money each month.

Eventually, they had enough that they could afford to build her a little shop between the house and mill house. There, she happily sold fine hats and dresses, though it was more to please her husband and sons than anything. For it really had been a girlish dream that was far outweighed by the joy of raising her sons.

Then, one fine autumn morning, the mother, now white-haired, was down to the river and came across the three stone figures buried in the bank. The memories they called up made her smile. She bent and began uncovering the face of one of them with her hands, beaming with pride at her husband's work, remembering how her boys had hurried out of the mill house with the stone figures that day and buried them here.

Ha! she thought, *What a big-hearted fool my husband is. After all these years, he still hasn't figured out how I tricked him.*

She was just about to bury the figures again when she noticed something in the arms of the sculpture of her eldest son. What on earth had her husband carved here? she wondered.

With a corner of her apron, she wiped away the sand and saw the stone face of an infant girl, as she lay asleep in her son's arms. For a moment she crouched there, not sure what she was seeing. Then she realized it was a gift of a daughter from her husband. By carving her here so perfectly, with every eyelash, every dimple on her little hands, he had hoped the old hag would bring her to life along with their boys.

She shook her head, thinking of all the months of work this must have taken. Then she remembered the box of toys and dresses from her childhood, up in the rafters. All this time, she'd thought she was the only one who cared that she had saved those old things. She sat there for the longest while, her hand caressing what her husband had made—with a little of her help—and her heart filled to overflowing. Had he felt this way when she brought their sons into the world? For surely, she'd never felt more loved.

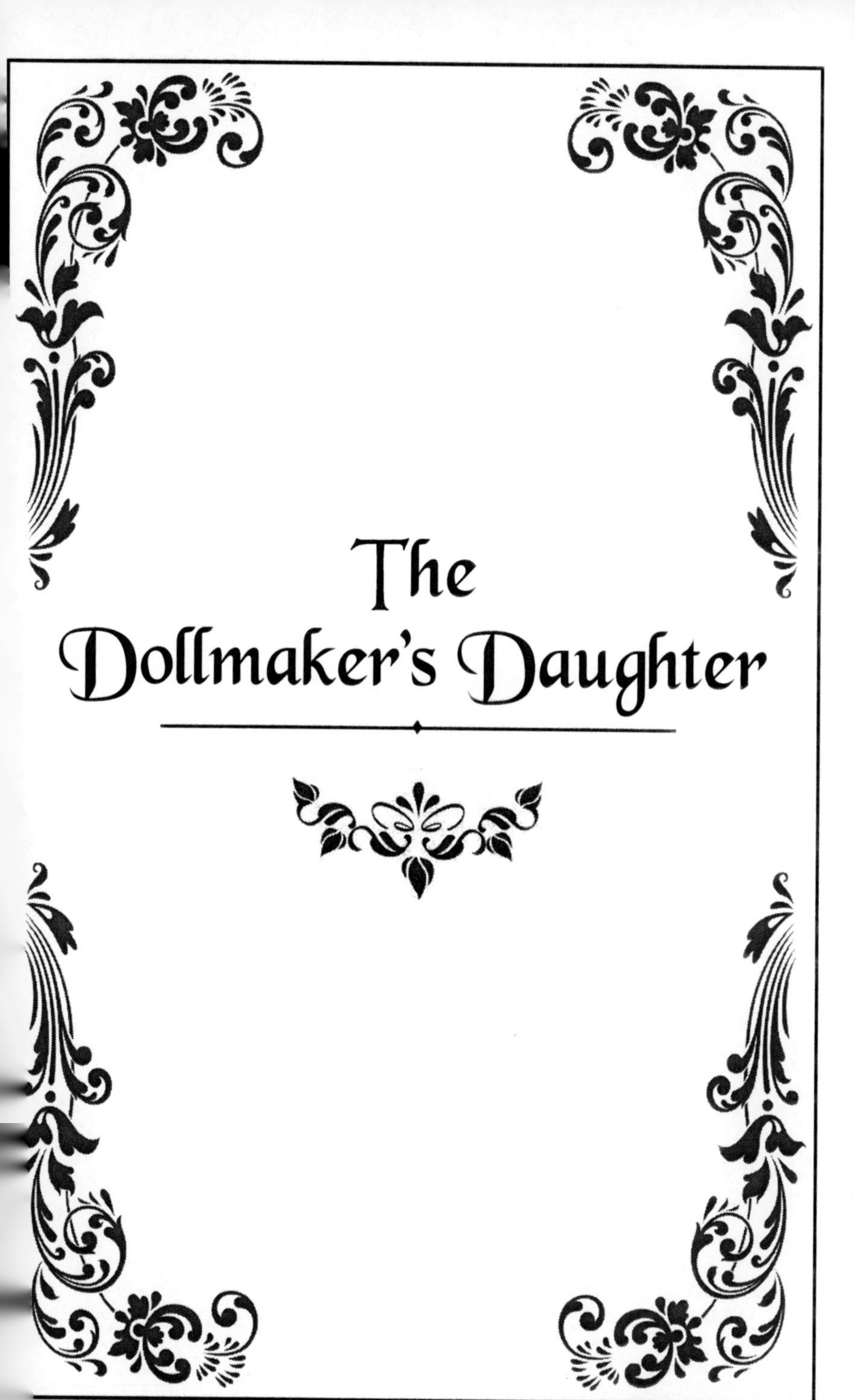

The Dollmaker's Daughter

The Dollmaker's Daughter

There were once two beautiful girls born to the queen of the land on the same night near Christmas. As the queen wanted only one girl, she told the midwife to take the other one away, hit it with a stick, and bury it under a tree in the woods.

With a heavy heart, the midwife hid the babe under her cloak and brought her down the back stairs, intending to go out by the kitchen door. But the cook stopped her, saying, "I know a young soldier and his wife who will gladly raise the child."

"Not a word of this to anyone," said midwife, passing the girl to her.

The cook took the squalling infant out into the snowy night, found the soldier's house, and the wife there took the girl in to raise as her own.

So while one sister was being given her first bath and wrapped in the finest silks and satins, the other girl, after she was wiped down with her new mother's apron, was wrapped in an old shirt made from nettles that grew in the soldier's yard.

Both fathers were away at war in the north when their girls arrived, fighting to win back a piece of land so harsh, more men died from weather than weapons. Both fathers received their happy news as the best of Christmas gifts. And both happened to send dolls home for their girls to play with, bought from travellers in a painted caravan who sold them foul-smelling cures for their wounded. But there the likeness between the fathers ended.

The soldier and his family were very poor. He sent most of his wages home, but it was far from enough for his wife and child live on. So in addition to all the usual backbreaking tasks of running a household, the wife took on sewing work, and sold wood she gathered from the forest where they lived. And when the soldier died out on the battlefield, firewood and sewing became her only sources of income.

The sights and sounds of the forest were the first memories for the soldier's daughter. As an infant, she was strapped to her mother's back and would play with her hair as they went in and out of the trees like a needle and thread. Later, when she began to sit up, her mother put her in the crook of a tree's roots while she combed the mossy floor. And later still, as soon as the girl was able to walk, her mother put her to work. Every stick that could be gathered in the forest meant another mouthful of porridge, and even the smallest child could gather sticks.

But one day, as the girl was at work in her small way, still within eyeshot of the house, a wolf caught her by the leg and carried her off. A keen-eyed hunter shot the wolf, but the girl's leg never recovered and had to be replaced by a wooden one, from the knee down.

Since she no longer dared let her girl go out into the woods, the mother taught her to spin and sew. The two of them copied the doll sent home from the war, making the body from wood found in the forest and the clothes from nettles in the yard. They sold these dolls in the town and made a little better living, but it was a hard life, working from morning to night, and the mother refused to let her daughter off easy. Many a night the girl would fall asleep over her sewing and her mother had to carry her to bed.

"Oh, my little one, I'm so sorry for making you work so hard," she said as she tucked the girl into her bed, "but if I died tomorrow, leaving you all crippled with no craft or skill—well, the wolf may as well have the rest of you."

Once in a while the girl managed to slip away to the forest, which she loved more than anything. There was one tree in particular she loved the most. It was the tallest one in the forest, a huge green spruce. She would play between its thick roots, making little dolls and a house for them out of twigs and moss. And there, in the flickering light under the spruce boughs, for a little while at least, she found some happiness.

Now, the story of the princess could not have been more different. The king, her father, was away at the war for the first four years of his daughter's life, and he never laid eyes on her in all that time. He was one of those large men who was afraid to be around delicate things, for it was only a matter of time before something was broken. So, since he had a gentle heart and a great deal of power, he would make others handle the delicate things and roar at them when they broke them.

Since he was keeping his kingdom safe, and since the queen was not large and didn't usually break things, he felt their daughter was in good hands. But the queen was from another country and he had married her, not because he loved her, but to stop a whole other war. He didn't know the queen didn't really like children. To her, their daughter was his daughter and since he wasn't there to roar at her, she spent her days trying not to become large like him.

Now, trying not to become large was especially difficult for the queen. She was a queen, after all, and if she wanted to she could eat mince pudding in the bath and put powdered sugar on everything. And that's exactly what she did. When she became larger than she liked, she would lock herself in her room for weeks on end and become thin again. Then she would start all over.

With the queen busy either eating or locked away, the servants found they had a great deal of time on their hands. During the first couple of months, they would do a little dusting or sweeping, and then go and play cards. But after years of this, they found the dusting and sweeping got in the way of their card playing, and so they stopped doing their work entirely.

As for the princess, the little girl toddled around, doing pretty much as she pleased. Before she could talk, when she wanted to be somewhere, she would get a servant to pick her up, then point where she wanted them to take her. In this way, she spent hours exploring the towers and the stables and tasting whatever the cook was making in the kitchen. She ate when she was hungry, slept where and when she liked, and dressed as she pleased. Though her room was never swept and her bed was falling down, it was full of dolls and toys that she loved very much.

The queen lost a great deal of sleep when she heard the king was coming home from the war. Her husband was a very neat, well-groomed man who hated filth and clutter, and the castle was not as tidy as it could have been. To prepare for the king's arrival, she ordered the servants to scrub the castle from the dungeons to the towers. But though they tried to sweep and clean as best they could, after so many years of card games and mince puddings, it was impossible to do everything. One of the things that they forgot was the princess.

The king arrived late at night, days earlier than everyone expected. He told the guards not to wake anyone and sent all of the servants back to bed. The castle seemed much smaller than he remembered, and he managed to knock a torch from the wall and tip over a huge vase within two steps of the front door. Worse, he was so glad to see his manservant that, when he shook his hand, he forgot his strength and nearly pulled the man's arm out of its socket.

The king had never met his daughter and after the torch nearly burned the place down and his manservant went away weeping, he was thankful it wasn't him taking care of his precious girl. As he went up the stairs, he imagined her room filled with elegant furniture and fine carpets that would be ruined by his huge boots. Perhaps he would just peek in the door. Would she still have that doll he sent her, after so many years?

But when he opened the door and held his candle high to peer in, he thought at first he was in the wrong room. Rats and bugs skittered away from the dried bread crusts and battered toys littering the floor. Then he saw the once elegant bed that was now broken from being jumped on. Around the bed were ragged dresses thrown here and there.

Was this some kind of joke?

In one corner stood an old Christmas tree, all of its needles fallen off. One of the servants had brought the tree in the year before for the little girl to decorate. The ornaments were faded and dusty, and spiders had made their webs among the branches. The king found his daughter curled beneath the tree, wrapped in a thin blanket. Her face and hands were covered in dust and soot from playing in the far corners of the castle. And there by the fire was the doll he had given her. Its features were long worn from its wooden head. Its dress was torn beyond repair and its hair was as snarled and matted as his daughter's.

The king felt his anger rise like a fire. This was a princess of the realm. This was his only daughter. He wanted to find whoever had done this, drag them up to the castle wall, and fling them to their death. How dare they treat his daughter like this!

But he restrained himself. He didn't want his daughter's first sight of him to be him killing all of the servants. He took a few deep breaths, trying to calm himself. He set the bed frame straight with a wooden box, then picked up the sleeping girl and lay her on the bed. Then he left the room and spoke to no one for the rest of the night.

The following day, he found out which servants were supposed to be taking care of his daughter and sent the three of them to the dungeon to sleep with the rats. The king then went from room to room, finding fault with everything in the castle. He ordered brooms, brushes, and buckets bought by the dozen and handed out to everyone. He then sent six new servants to clear his daughter's room to the bare walls, and burn everything removed. It took two weeks to scrub the castle to the king's satisfaction.

The queen kept to her chambers, fearing the wrath of the king. He refused to speak to her about their daughter or the filthy state of the castle, so she had no opportunity to apologize.

The little princess didn't understand why everything was changing, now that her father was home. The king couldn't stand the sight of dolls or toys after seeing all the broken ones, so she was not allowed to have any at all. New dresses were bought for her and she was cinched into them till her back was so straight, she couldn't bend to do up her own shoes. Her hair was brushed and put into tight braids. And her face and hands were powdered so that she looked as if she'd been in the kitchen, playing catch with the bread dough.

Needless to say, the princess hated all the new rules. She wanted her toys back and didn't understand why they'd been taken away. But she tried her best not to cry when the servants combed her matted hair. And even though her dresses and her shoes and her braids all pinched, she was told she was a brave girl and given sweets when she behaved.

Now, the next three years passed so quickly, you'd think a thief had stolen them away. The queen tolerated about a year of her husband's large ways. He filled the royal table with roast pigs, endless cups of ale, and his loud war stories. He filled her bed, their bed, with his great big self and kept elbowing her in the middle of the night. He even filled one of her favourite rooms at the front of the castle with his war trophies, his swords and his armour. Where was there room for her?

So when the queen's father, who lived in a distant kingdom, fell ill, she nearly ran to the waiting carriage to go and care for him. As it turned out, she caught the same illness that had afflicted him. Her stomach bloated like a cow's udder, her eyes grew as sunken as a skeleton's. She aged forty years in as many weeks and ended up dying just as her father recovered.

The king was quite aware that he knew nothing about raising a child and that he had wiped away everything familiar to his daughter. But he was confident he could do much better than the queen and the servants had done. He had managed large armies, after all. How difficult could it be to care for a little girl?

He decided to treat her as he had been treated by his own nursemaid when he was a little boy. She had always been clear, strong and fair with him and never raised her voice, even when he broke any of the rich and beautiful things in his room. Patient and strict as his nurse was, he loved and admired her to this day, even if he was still a little afraid of her.

Straight away, the king filled his daughter's room with beautiful furniture and tapestries and never missed a chance to buy her things. Clothes and shoes were the easiest and, he felt, the most pleasing. But he also bought her brushes for her hair, fine gloves for her little hands, and expensive carpets for her floor.

Gifts often arrived at the castle gates for the princess from well-wishers and distant relatives. But the king would have his manservant open them first to make sure that he approved, then wrap them up again. If there were toys or other childish baubles, he would replace them with practical things, then in his reply letter he'd thank the sender for the thing he had tossed out the kitchen window.

To the princess, her father was both a mystery and a great source of resentment. They sat beside each other every evening at the vast table in the great hall. And every evening was the same. He would compliment her on her hair or clothes. She would thank him, then they would sit there, eating in silence for the rest of the meal. *Why sit together if you aren't going to talk?* she wondered.

Then there were the proclamations. Whenever he had to give a speech to the people, he would have her put on a special red and gold silk dress and have her hair braided in just a certain way. Then she had to stand with him like a statue on the balcony before all the people and smile, even though she hated to.

The princess soon grew tired of tight braids and tight dresses. Even at night, she was tucked into bed with the sheets pulled so stiff her toes bent down like the heads of ducks. She wasn't in his army, she thought. Why did she have to be so perfect all the time? She longed for the days when she could wear what she pleased and go where she wished. And soon she found a way.

In a corner of the kitchen, the cook kept a box of rags for cleaning up spills. The princess found an old dress and coat in the rag box and would change into them to sneak out of the castle. She would put a cap on her head and a little soot on her face and off she'd go out the kitchen door.

The forest beyond the town was a vast thing. The floor of it was easy to walk, because people were always picking up sticks for firewood. She had heard that many people hunted game there, but she rarely came across any of them. There, she could be free. There was no one to tell her what to wear or how to smile. And after dozens of visits to the forest, she found a place where no one would bother her.

A great spruce tree grew in the middle of the forest. A thick cushion of needles and moss covered the ground beneath it. It always reminded her of the Christmas tree the servants had once put in her room and let her decorate. When it rained or snowed she could sit under the tree and stay dry and watch the world outside. And more than once she had fallen asleep under it.

Between two big roots, someone had built a little house from twigs and moss and filled it with skillfully-made little dolls. As the princess was not allowed dolls or any other toys in the castle, she relished this chance to play with them and always wondered about the person who put them there.

Then one day as she was leaving the tree, she heard singing far behind her in the woods. Fearing it might be someone from the castle, she hid herself and waited to see who it was. Just as she was safely out of sight, she saw another girl approaching the great tree. She was about the same height and age as the princess. Her hair was under a cap and she seemed to have something wrong with one leg, for she was limping.

The princess watched her play under the great tree for some time, as the forest floor was quite clear, and she was not sure she could get away home without being seen. So at the risk of being very late, she stayed until the other girl got up to leave.

Now she was overcome with curiosity. She followed the girl through the woods till they came to a little house in a clearing with dark trees rising sharply around it. She could see hens pecking in the yard and a cat playing on the doorstep. When the other girl went inside the house, she crept closer and saw dolls and parts of dolls hanging in the window. *They must make them here*, she thought. How lucky that girl was!

The cat came around the corner of the house just then and began to meow at her and brush itself against her legs. Afraid she'd be found out, she hurried away, thinking what a wonderful life that other girl had, surrounded by happy things.

The princess was very late getting back to the castle, and the cook wagged a wooden spoon at her as she came in the door. She changed out of her rags as quickly as she could and hurried to the great hall for dinner.

When she arrived at her place at the table, she quickly discovered that everyone in the castle had been looking for her. The servants, even the soldiers had been told to drop what they were doing and search high and low. Three guards had already been sent to the dungeon to sleep with the rats for returning to the great hall without her.

"Where have you been?" her father asked gruffly.

The princess was not about to reveal the truth, so she answered simply, "Playing."

This did not sit well with the king. Not wanting to yell at his daughter, he kept his words short and to the point. "Playing? We'll have no more of that. If the servants cannot keep you out of trouble, I'll find someone who can."

The princess was sent to bed after only two bites of supper, as she was too upset to eat any more. She lay there for what seemed hours, shaken by her father's anger but unable to stop thinking about the girl in the woods with all the dolls.

The next day, the king did find someone whom he

hoped would keep the princess out of trouble. Midmorning, an old woman appeared in the great hall with a small bag of her possessions. She had more lines on her face than a breadboard and a wart on one side of her chin. The old woman had been the king's own nursemaid when he was a little boy and raised him till he was nearly a teenager. The guards had never seen their ruler bow to anyone before, but he bowed now.

"Thank you for agreeing to care for my daughter," said the king, who stood there looking like he was ten years old again. "I need someone with a kind heart and firm hand for the girl."

"Thank you, Your Majesty," said the new nursemaid. "I will keep you informed of your daughter's progress. If I see a need to change things, I will always seek instruction."

The nursemaid was shown to her room by one of the servants and began her duties bright and early the next morning.

From the first plait of the first braid, the princess knew she was going to like this old woman. The braid wasn't tight at all, and yet it looked beautiful in the mirror. But when she felt her hair with a hand, her happiness turned to fear. "I cannot go out like this," she said to her new nurse.

"And why not?" asked the old woman. "Not a hair is out of place."

"Father will be angry. You must make my braids tighter."

The old woman rolled her eyes. Then she sat the girl down and redid her braids as tight as she dared without hurting her. "How is that?" she asked.

The girl looked in the mirror, but was afraid to say anything. The nurse knew immediately she had not done a good enough job. "If I make your hair any tighter, your head will surely ache."

"It always aches," said the princess. "That's how I know my hair is done up right."

The old woman's eyes went wide. "Bah!" she said. "A pox on that!" and before the girl could say another word the nurse was gone out the door.

She marched into the great hall and stood before the king. "Your daughter's hair is kept much too tight," she said. "If it is not loosened, the girl will surely suffer permanent harm."

The king was sitting sharpening a sword he'd brought from his trophy room. He looked up calmly and said, "You have only begun taking care of my daughter. You don't understand what is important. She spent years without cleanliness or order and now must spend years to correct that. The harm was done long ago. This is now the cure."

The old woman saw that the king was not going to budge. "Thank you, Your Majesty," she said, and out she went, muttering to herself.

A little while later, the nurse was doing up the girl's dress. She was nearly finished when she saw the princess giving her that look in the mirror. "Don't tell me this has to be done up tighter."

"I'm sorry," said the princess.

So the nurse cinched the dress till her own fingers turned purple. "How is that?"

But she could tell immediately it was still not tight enough. "If I make your dress any tighter, you won't be able to get a breath."

"I can never get a breath," said the princess. "That's how I know my dress is done up right."

"Bah! A pox on that!" said the old woman, and off to see the king she went.

"Your daughter's dresses are kept much too tight," she said. "If they are not loosened, the girl will surely suffer permanent harm."

The king was picking meat out of his teeth with an enormous knife. He gave her a small smile and answered calmly, "The harm was done long ago. This is now the cure."

Frustrated as she was, the old woman bit her tongue and left with a polite smile.

A short while later, the nurse was painting the girl's lips and powdering her face. "What are all these red spots here?" asked the nurse. "You've got them all over your forehead and neck."

"Don't worry," said the girl. "That always happens. The powder stings my skin. Just put a little more on to cover up the red spots."

"Bah!" said the old woman. "A pox on that!" And out the door she went. She didn't care what answer she got from the king; but she needed to give him a piece of her left eye.

"Your daughter's makeup is making her break out in spots," she said. "If she has to continue wearing it, the girl will surely suffer a permanent injury."

The king had a great big battleaxe across his lap, trying to see if he could get the bloodstains off with his thumbnail. "You know what I'm going to say," he answered calmly. "Nothing has changed."

The old woman made sure she leveled her left eye at the king for a good long while. "Thank you, Your Majesty," she said coldly.

Then one day, as the nurse was braiding the princess's hair, trying to make it as tight as the girl wanted it, she said, "Now, I know this hurts. You can't tell me it doesn't. What I don't know is, how do you stand it?"

"Oh," said the girl, looking down at her hands. "It's only for a short while. When I get big I'm going to run away forever."

The old woman was both amused and concerned. "Don't you like being a princess?"

"No," the girl said matter-of-factly. "It's too much trouble. I just want to live in a little house that is filled with—" She didn't want to say dolls, knowing how her father hated them, so she said, "Simple things."

Of all the matters the old nurse spoke to the king about, this was one she never mentioned. It would crush the poor man to know how his daughter felt about her role. But that didn't stop her wanting to make things better for the girl. And she kept going to the king almost daily with fresh complaints.

The king always listened to the nurse, for he had great respect for her, but for all her wasted breath, he never changed a thing. In fact, matters became worse over time. For now that the king had a reliable caretaker for his girl, he began giving more orders, knowing she would carry them out.

For instance, he wanted his girl to walk straighter, as she had a tendency to lean forward from her headaches and tight dress. So he had the old woman make her walk with a book on her head. And when that kept falling off, he had the nurse tie a broomstick to her back and braids and make the girl walk around with that for an hour every afternoon.

Then one day, as the nurse was fetching tea from the kitchen, she noticed a local tradesman at the door. He had brought his child with him and the child was playing with a small toy.

"I just realized something," said the nurse. "Where are all the princess's toys?"

"Ssh!" the cook quietened her. Then, looking to see if anyone was listening, she whispered, "I'm surprised you don't know. She's not allowed to have any."

Every wrinkle on the old woman's face began to twist in disbelief. "Pardon me?"

The cook did her best to explain why. She was not even finished the story when the old nurse put the tea tray down with a bang. "What a sad thing this is!"

"That's not the half of it," said the cook with a shake of her head.

"What do you mean?" the nurse asked.

The cook tugged at her sleeve. "Come with me."

She brought the nurse around to the back of the fireplace where there was a door to a large pantry. In they went with a candle, and the nurse's eyes went wide. The whole back of the room was filled with toys and boxes. The nurse ran her eyes over hobby horses and marionettes and animals made from silk and fine spun wool, some with the ribbons still around their necks.

"Any gift that comes to the front door, if he doesn't like it, it gets thrown out the back. I couldn't just leave them there on the ash heap, such beautiful things."

"How long has this been going on?"

"Years," said the cook.

The old woman scowled for a moment, then spat, "Bah! A pox on that!"

"What are you going to do?" asked the cook.

"Oh, you just wait and see," said the nurse.

After that, the next time the old nurse ran into the king, she gave a happy sigh as she looked away from him.

"What are you sighing about?" the king asked.

"Oh," said his old nurse, "I was just remembering when you were a little boy. You were such a sweet lad and your father was so good to you. Remember those beautiful toy soldiers he had made for you one year? He was so proud of them and you loved them so much."

The king said nothing, and gave her a small nod.

The next time she met him, she sighed again and talked about the hobby horse the king had when he was little. "You're lucky you had such a good father. He'd watch you ride that hobby horse up and down and up and down the great hall. Oh, he used to laugh."

This time, the king cracked a smile.

The nurse kept at him for the next several weeks, each time reminding him of some happy childhood event and how good his father was to him. Then one day she came to him and said, "Remember when you were small and I'd tuck you into bed with all your toys? You were so sweet. You said you couldn't get to sleep without all your little friends to protect you."

The king smiled broadly and shook his head. "That was a long time ago."

"Indeed, it was," said his old nurse. "By the way, Christmas is fast approaching. Have you thought about a gift for the princess?"

The king was taken aback. "I...yes, I have," he fumbled.

"Well," said his old nurse, "I hope it's the sort of gift a good father would give."

The king spent a restless night, thinking about what his old nurse had said. The truth was, he had planned to give his daughter new curtains for her room. But he was now reconsidering. He knew curtains were not exactly something a child would want. And of course, he wanted to be a good father to her at Christmas. But dare he open that old wound and give her some plaything a seven year old would like? What if something should go wrong?

He sat up in bed. By the glow from the room's fireplace, he remembered that night when he came home from the war and found his girl living in filth and disarray. What a horrible night that was! But years had now passed. He knew perfectly well how to make his daughter happy. What was stopping him was lack of courage. Cost what it may, he decided, he had to show courage and put his own past injuries aside.

Bright and early the following morning, the king called for his manservant. When the man arrived, he said to him, "I have been reconsidering my gift for the princess."

"I see," said his servant. "But the new curtains for her room will arrive tomorrow."

"Forget about that," said the king. "I have changed my mind. I want you to go out and buy—" The king stopped, as if something were sticking in his throat.

"Yes, Your Majesty?"

"I want you to buy one of every...toy you can find in the kingdom."

His servant couldn't stop blinking. "Yes, Your Majesty. But did you want, um...every toy?"

The king looked at him carefully. "You're asking about a doll?"

"Yes, Your Majesty."

The king took a deep breath and rubbed his brow for a moment. Then he said, "Fine. But not any doll. You must find the most beautiful doll in the kingdom. Nothing else will do."

This being such an important subject for the king, the servant tried to get details. His own nieces had many dolls and were very particular about their style. "Should it be carved or stuffed?" he asked the king. "Should the arms and legs bend? And if so, should they use pins or hinges?"

"I don't know the answers to any of that," said the king with a wave of his hand. "Go ask the girl's nursemaid."

The servant began bowing and backing his way toward the door. "Thank you, Your Majesty. I will speak to her and begin placing orders immediately."

"Wait!" the king blurted, stopping him. "You must let me know when the doll arrives. I want to see that it is suitable for the princess."

His servant bowed and hurried out. He was so excited about this change in the king that he couldn't help telling the happy news to everyone he encountered on his way to see the nursemaid. "Can you believe it? Not just toys, but a doll, too! It's incredible!"

The old woman was in the princess's chambers. When he brought her out to ask her advice, he did not get the reaction he expected. "Pins or hinges? Bah! No one cares. The poor girl is starving and you're worried she won't like cake. Calm down, man. She'll love whatever you get her."

That afternoon, the manservant began asking everyone in the castle if they knew where he might find toys or a doll in such a short amount of time. There were, by then, only five days until Christmas. Some people spoke of a toymaker in a distant village, others of a farmer who sometimes sold things he had carved. But everyone, down to a man, spoke of the soldier's wife who lived in the woods not far away.

The cook said to him, "You'll not find a better doll anywhere. All the girls in the town want one. And she's started making them in red and gold dresses, just like the princess wears. The girls see her up on the balcony during the king's speeches and want a doll just like that."

"Perfect," said the servant. The cook gave him directions to the dollmaker's little house in the woods and later that day, he found it without any trouble.

When the dollmaker heard the knock and saw a strange man on her doorstep, she put her daughter in the cupboard before opening the door.

The man stood holding his hat in his hands. "I am here on the king's behalf," he said. "I would like to order the biggest, finest doll you can make. The one in red and gold. But it has to be more beautiful than any other."

The dollmaker chuckled. "Are you playing a joke on me? I thought the king hated dolls."

The servant beamed. "He has changed his mind. And when you are done, there will be a tidy bag of silver to prove it."

When the servant left, the dollmaker got her girl out of the cupboard and the two did a little dance, thinking how much money this commission would bring to their household. They began work immediately, the mother carving and painting the body of the doll, the girl sewing the dress.

As Christmas neared, the dollmaker's girl worked hard, for they had many dolls to finish and not much time to do it. Whenever the girl looked up from her sewing, she saw the trees out the window, all beautifully covered in snow, and she longed to be out there.

One day, while her mother was away delivering dolls meant as gifts for other girls in the town, she couldn't help herself—and snuck out to her tree in the woods. It had been many weeks since she had been able to slip away, and to celebrate Christmas, she made a new stick doll and dressed it in red and gold scraps she had picked up from the floor at home. She poked a twig she broke from one of the branches overhead into the moss as a miniature Christmas tree for her doll to celebrate under. Then she hurried home, dreading the long hours of work ahead of her.

The following day, two days before Christmas, with the everyone distracted by the holiday, the princess found her own chance to sneak away. Down the back stairs she went to the kitchen, where she changed into her ragged dress and coat while the cook was busy elsewhere. Then, as quietly as she could, she went out the kitchen door and made her way to the woods.

It had snowed heavily again the night before. The forest was very still and great puffs of snow lay upon every branch, making the hollow beneath her favourite tree seem all the more safe and secret. She found the miniature tree the other girl had poked into the moss. But she was very surprised by the red and gold dress on the little twig doll she had left there. Was this a gift from the other girl? Did the other girl know she was the princess, or that she was visiting the tree too? She was suddenly overcome by excitement—she might make a friend!

She didn't want to move the little doll in case it wasn't meant for her. And she knew she couldn't take it back to the castle anyway. But as she ran home through the snow, she vowed to return with a gift for the other girl.

Come Christmas Eve, the king's manservant was nearly out of his mind with worry. Early in the week he had sent twelve men out to the towns and countryside to find toys that were worthy of the princess. But everything they brought back was either beautiful and poorly made or well-made and ugly. Worse, the king kept asking him, sometimes twice a day, to check on the progress of the doll. Was it ready yet? What was taking them so long? The manservant kept sending a pageboy out to the little house in the woods and understandably, the lad was getting tired of slogging through the snow. And though he didn't know it, the dollmaker's daughter was getting tired of being put in the cupboard.

"What am I to do?" he lamented, within earshot of the princess's old nurse. "The king growled at me again this morning. I have only three little toys that are worthy of the princess."

"I believe I can help you," said the nurse.

She brought the manservant down to the kitchen and around to the pantry and showed him the gifts the king had thrown out over the years.

"I don't care where they came from," said the servant. "These are beautiful. Thank you. You have saved me from the dungeon—or worse." He got the pageboy to help him carry all the gifts out of the pantry, then dusted them off and made sure they had new bows.

The king was worried, flustered and excited about Christmas Eve. Not wanting any of his surprises spoiled, he had the princess sent to bed early. But it was anything but early when she got to sleep that night.

She couldn't stop thinking about the girl in the woods and the little stick doll in red and gold she'd left. The moment her nurse tucked her in and hobbled from her chambers, she crept out of bed and checked the door. Then she hurried down the back stairs to the rag box in the kitchen. She had a Christmas gift for that other girl in the forest and she was determined to deliver it, come what may. It was a small pin that had belonged to her mother, shaped like a royal crown with three little gemstones in it.

Once she was changed, she crept across the stone floor as quietly as she could. The kitchen door was bolted and she was afraid it would make too much noise to open it, so she went out the window where they threw the kitchen garbage and ash from the fire.

She had never been out in the forest at night. It was cold and clear, with the moon and stars lighting her way. The snow crunched underfoot and she could hear wolves howling in the distance.

In the middle of the forest, she heard voices, and hid behind a snow-covered bush. It turned out, it was only an old man passing by, singing a Christmas song to himself as he dragged a small sleigh full of firewood. Once he was out of sight and she could no longer hear his song, she continued on.

But when she arrived at the tree, she received a terrible shock. She thought at first she had taken a wrong turn in the dark, for all she found was a stump about knee high and white chips of wood from the work of an axe all around. The twig house and its little people were trampled into the moss and the whole place smelled of cut wood instead of green boughs. The girl tried her best not to cry, as much for the beautiful tree as for the happy times she had spent under its boughs.

She made her way home through the snow, quite heartsick, feeling as cold and poor as she looked in her rags. When she arrived back at the kitchen window, which she'd left open a crack to let herself back in, it glowed with a light burning inside. She saw the king's manservant sitting with the cook over tea.

Not wanting to be discovered, she went all the way around to the front of the castle and in through the courtyard, shivering with every step. The guard there was drunk and sound asleep, so she was able to sneak by him and creep up the steps and into the great hall. By then, she was so tired and cold, she didn't care who saw her in her ragged coat and dress.

And then she saw the tree, standing upright in a corner of the great hall. It was the biggest Christmas tree she had ever laid eyes on, with a huge velvet cloth beneath it covered in gifts, big and small. The whole room smelled of the sap and greenness of the fresh-cut tree. It was decorated with dried flowers, ribbons and great garlands of small apples and berries, some red, some painted gold.

She had been brave in the forest and not cried for her tree. But now there was no helping it. She lay down at its foot, just as she used to lie beneath it in the forest, and sobbed and sobbed till she cried herself into the deepest of sleeps.

At the dollmaker's house, the girl and her mother were almost finished their work. The mother had hung the wooden body of the doll from a cord by the fire, hoping the paint would dry in time.

"I have to make two more deliveries," she said to her girl. "I hope you'll be done sewing by the time I get back." And off she went into the night.

The moment her mother was out the door, the daughter took a little rest. She had been working on the dress since she'd awakened that morning and her hands were sore. It was the largest dress they had ever made, and it took far more work than usual. She played with the house cat for a little while, then fell asleep in her chair. The next thing she knew, she was startled by her mother's cry as she shook her awake.

"I'm almost done!" the girl said.

"It's you and I who are done!" said the mother.

The girl looked around, wondering what she was talking about. Her eyes fell first on the cat, who was sitting up on the mantle by the chimney. Then she saw the broken cord and the wooden body of the doll lying in the fire, burning brightly.

The mother rushed to pull it out of the fire, but it was finished, and she sat down on the floor and laughed till she cried. "Now what are we to do? I just hope the king doesn't put us in chains."

"At least we still have the dress," said the girl.

The dress was draped across the girl's lap and her mother's eyes saw the wooden leg sticking out of it. "That's it!" she said. "You've given me an idea. Put the dress on, girl. This may be our only hope of saving ourselves."

The girl tipped her head and frowned. She didn't know what her mother meant.

"I will paint your face and you can pretend to be a doll at the castle for a few days. Just until I have time to make another body. Then we'll put the wooden doll in the dress and you can come home."

The girl was happy her mother wasn't angry with her. And she was doubly happy to be able to wear the fancy dress all day.

"But you will have to be still as a piece of wood," warned her mother. "Do you think you can do that?"

The girl's eyes were wide with excitement as she nodded. She was going to live in a castle!

An hour later, the dollmaker arrived at the kitchen door of the castle with a large box across her arms.

"At last!" cried the manservant, and he and the cook helped her carry it to the table. "My goodness, it's heavy," he said.

Once they'd set it down, he nudged the dollmaker aside, undid the bow, and lifted the top of the box. "Well, they were right. I've never seen such a beautiful doll before."

The cook had not seen the woman since that night, long ago, when she had brought the babe to her house out in the woods. The moment she looked into the box, her eyes went wide and she started coughing to hide her surprise.

"What's this?" the manservant exclaimed. "The legs aren't the same at all. One's all smooth and painted and the other's still rough and wooden-looking."

The dollmaker rubbed her cold hands nervously. "I'm so sorry, I promise to replace it right away. But I had no time!"

The servant shook his head. "That's no excuse. But there's nothing we can do tonight." And he put the lid back on and retied the bow. "Be gone now," he said to the dollmaker. "I'll pay you when you finish that leg."

The dollmaker went back out into the cold night, worried sick about her girl. Tired as she was, she was determined not sleep until she had made a new body for the doll.

In the kitchen, the manservant began to panic. "What am I going to do? I can't let the king see the doll like this!"

"Well," the cook said calmly, "perhaps the dollmaker can finish the other leg by morning. In the meantime, let's hide the box in the pantry so no one sees it."

So the two carried the box into the pantry and closed the door. When the manservant was gone, the cook grabbed a few biscuits and a cup of tea from the table and hurried back to the pantry.

"How did this happen, little one?" she asked as the girl sat up, happily accepting tea and biscuits.

The girl told the cook all about falling asleep and how the cat had knocked the body of the doll into the fire.

"Don't you worry, dear," said the cook. "Everything will be alright." And when the girl was done her tea and biscuits, the cook told her to go to sleep. "I'll be right outside if you need anything."

Not everything was alright for the manservant, however. He went up to the king's bedchamber to report, his knees quivering with fear over what he was going to say.

"Is the doll finished?" the king asked him, when he sheepishly opened the door.

The manservant had to be honest. "Yes and no, Your Majesty."

"Well, is it here?"

"Most of it, Your Majesty."

"Is it more beautiful than any other doll in the kingdom?"

"I hope so, Your Majesty."

The king had had about enough of this. "Get out of my sight!" he shouted. "I will see for myself."

"You can't!" the manservant blurted.

The king towered over him and his glare was enough to make the servant scurry from the room, wondering if he should pack his bags and run away before he was thrown into the dark dungeon, or worse.

As soon as he was gone, the king pulled on a cloak and barged out of the room. *Something is wrong*, he thought. Why else would his manservant behave like that?

He descended the stairs and crossed the great hall, looking up at the huge tree he had ordered and had decorated for his daughter. Only the biggest and best tree was good enough for her. But now, wondering what it was that his manservant didn't want him to see, he looked around the tree with suspicion. What were all these toys and boxes under its boughs? Suddenly he recognized some of them. These were things he had thrown out, he realized, back when he was so horrified by his daughter's condition. All the hurtful memories came flooding back and his hand went to his heart. Then his eye fell on the girl in rags that had fallen asleep among the gifts. And his heart nearly stopped.

Well, well, he thought. *Here is what they think of me. Dressing up a doll in rags.* Everyone knew the story of him returning from the war to find his daughter under the old Christmas tree in a ragged dress and a threadbare blanket. But what a cruel joke this was now. Surely this was the work of that old nurse of his. "She's mocking me," he muttered angrily.

The king picked up what he thought was a doll, strode across the great hall, and down the steps to the kitchen. He marched across the room and with one kick he sent the wooden window flying open and threw the doll onto the garbage pile outside.

"How dare you mock me!" he shouted. Then he slammed the window shut, whirled, and stomped out of the kitchen.

Two minutes later, still purple with fury, the king was back in his room. He called for his manservant and paced back and forth, trying to calm himself enough to speak when the man arrived. When his servant finally appeared, the king did his best to control himself. "I have been downstairs and I have seen that horrid doll."

The servant immediately thought the king had been to the kitchen and seen the doll with the mismatched legs. "I-I'm sorry, Your Majesty. I tried my best to have it ready in time."

"Whose idea was it to make the doll look like that? Did you speak to the nursemaid about it?"

"Why, yes, Your Majesty. But—"

"And all those other things under the tree," roared the king. "I suppose she had a hand in that?"

"Well, yes, but all she did was show me where—"

"Go and fetch her immediately!" the king bellowed.

The servant bowed and hurried from the king's chambers. It took some time to rouse the old woman from her bed and bring her before the king. The servant could tell the king's anger had not subsided, for as they entered the room, he was still pacing, furiously.

The king was extremely curt with the nursemaid. "You are dismissed from service. Pack your bags and get out."

The old woman stood staring at the king for a moment. Then she shrugged and turned to go.

But the king was not finished. "You and your loose braids, your lax ways, and your hideous doll," he said. "You're just an old witch. Putting ideas into my daughter's head. Plotting against me."

The nurse stopped. Then she turned just enough to see the king out of the corner of her eye. "I'm an old witch, am I?" she said. "Well, here's a spell for you. You have a flesh and blood girl here and yet you are turning her into a doll, button by button, braid by braid. Without me, soon there will be no girl left, you mark my words."

The king waved a hand and his manservant took the old woman away. Her bags were packed that night and she was sent out of the castle gates into the snow.

When the princess found herself on the pile of ashes and vegetable peelings, she had no idea how she got there. She had heard her father's voice shouting, but what did he mean? Was he the one who had thrown her outside? She had been awakened from her slumber with such a start, she was up and out of the ash heap almost before the window was slammed behind her. What if it was her father? What was she to do?

Needing a moment to think, and not wanting to freeze there in the snow, she hurried down the lane to the stables. She went inside the first stall she came to and sat between the legs of an old horse there, who was lying on his side, asleep. The warmth and smell of him made her cry again and she decided if she could manage to sleep herself, she might think clearer in the morning.

She slept until just before sunrise between the legs of the big, warm horse. She was still hurt and confused about what had happened the night before. They'd cut down her favourite tree and when she fell asleep under it, her father got angry and threw her out. What was she to do now? She couldn't bear to go back inside the castle. Maybe it was time to run away, even if she wasn't big yet.

The old horse stood up when she did, though he had trouble doing it. He was much smaller than she thought he'd be. He was black, with a matted mane and hooves so overgrown, he looked like he was wearing shoes. It was plain he was an old toll pony, which people sometimes brought to pay their taxes with if they had no money. She found a rope halter and he bowed his head when she put in on.

From the ash heap, she filled her pockets with turnip peelings and off down the road she went on the toll pony, past all the doors with Christmas ribbons and pine boughs over them, wondering where she could go.

Every Christmas morning since the king had returned from the war, he gave a speech from the castle balcony. Baskets of fruit and nuts were given out to the people who came to listen, so most of the townspeople showed up.

The king always dressed in his finest robes and made sure his crown was perfectly polished for the occasion. His daughter always wore her special red and gold silk dress and stood on a chair so the people could see her better. Only this morning, when the maids went in to get the girl ready for the day, she was not in her bed.

Word quickly spread among the other maids and servants. Everyone hurried about the castle, searching for the girl. Word of her nurse being fired the night before had spread quickly, and they were all afraid of losing their job or being sent to the dungeon to sleep with the rats if they couldn't find the princess. She had done this before, run off and hidden herself because she didn't want to get dressed up for her father's speech. But this morning, with only minutes before she was to be ready, they still hadn't found her.

In his frantic search, one of the servants went tearing into the kitchen. The cook was nowhere to be seen for, busy as she was with the king's breakfast, she'd noticed the old coat and dress missing from the rag box and gone out back to look for the girl. The servant peered into every cupboard and looked under every table. Finally he flung open the door of the pantry. Now, the cook had told the girl that if she heard anyone coming, she was to jump into the box and stay as still as she could. And that is just how the servant found her.

"Well, look at this!" he said. "They must have been planning a special surprise. This is just like the doll I gave my own girl this morning, only it's much bigger. That dollmaker is a wonder."

The servant got a blanket and hid the doll under it. Then he carried it upstairs to where the king had already begun giving his Christmas speech on the balcony.

"What are you doing?" asked one of the guards.

"Look here," said the servant, lifting the blanket. "The king will never know. The poor girl just stands there every year like a doll anyway. She never has to say anything."

"You're mad," said the guard. "If the king finds out, they're going to dig the dungeon deeper just for you."

Even so, he helped the servant remove the blanket. Then they parted the curtain to the balcony and propped the doll up on the chair behind the king for all the people to see.

As soon as the girl was put out there, a great cheer rose from the people down below. The king turned, saw his daughter was bright-eyed and smiling, and continued his speech.

It was the king's habit to speak far too long every year. Once everyone had been given their gift baskets, they all wanted to leave. But the guards closed the courtyard gates behind them, so they all had to stand there and listen. After a little while, one of the servants went down to the courtyard to stand with his wife. He gave her a wink and whispered, "You'll never guess what's going on up there. They couldn't find the princess this morning, so they put a doll up there in her place."

"No!" exclaimed his wife. "You're joking."

"I'm not," said the servant. "Just you watch and see if she blinks."

His wife studied the princess carefully. "You're right," she said after a minute. "She's not moving a hair." And she nudged her neighbor and whispered for her to look.

Soon the whole courtyard was whispering and pointing at the doll set up on the balcony."Look at her. Does he think we're fools not to notice?"

The sound of the people grew so loud, the king paused, wondering what all the commotion was about.

"It's a doll!" someone yelled up at him. "Look, it's not the princess, it's just a doll!"

When the king heard this, he had no idea what they were talking about. He glanced around at the girl on the chair behind him. She looked the same as she always did in her red and gold dress, her face powdered and her lips painted. But when he turned back, his eyes fell on a hunched figure in the crowd down below. It was his old nursemaid. And suddenly he remembered what she had said to him: "*You're turning your daughter into a doll, button by button, braid by braid. Soon there will be no girl left, you mark my words.*"

A cold chill went up the king's spine. Since he'd been a little boy, he had always felt the power of this woman over him. Now, all wrinkled and bent, she looked even more like a witch, standing down there with her crooked smile. He turned again to look at his daughter. And this time he saw the wooden leg and ankle and another chill swept over him.

"My dear," he managed to say. "Can you give the crowd a little wave?"

The servant behind the curtain cringed, thinking his trick would be found out when the doll couldn't wave.

The crowd continued taunting the king. "Look at her! You should be ashamed of yourself! It's just a doll!"

The king gave a smile to the crowd and waved to them himself. "Please, girl," he said. "I beg of you, give them a little wave."

At that moment, the girl on the chair slowly raised her right arm and waved stiffly. The crowd fell silent. But back behind the balcony curtain, the servant fainted dead away, thinking the doll had come to life.

The king was pleased that his daughter's wave had reassured the people. But he was so distracted by the girl's apparently wooden leg, he cut his speech short and helped her down from her chair. The servant had recovered by then, and held the curtains apart for the king and the princess, his eyes wide as saucers, seeing the doll walking.

Hearing the *clunk, clunk* of the little girl's wooden foot on the stone floor, the king found he couldn't breathe for a moment. She's been cursed, he thought. *The old nursemaid has cursed my daughter.*

Holding her little hand, the king led the girl down the stairs to the great hall, where Christmas breakfast was being served. As soon as the girl saw the huge Christmas tree in the corner, she recognized it immediately. Though she tried her best not to cry, holding this big, strange man's hand, she couldn't help it.

The king thought her wooden leg must be hurting her and held her hand all the tighter.

The girl wiped her eyes and took a big breath. *I must be brave*, she thought, *or they'll discover who I am and they'll be angry with me.*

The king sat the girl down beside him and made sure she was quite comfortable. Then he drank a full cup of ale in one long draught, and stared off into space, not knowing what to think. With the girl sitting, her wooden leg stuck straight out in front of her. *This is my doing*, thought the king. *The nurse has done nothing but tell the future. This is all my doing.*

In the kitchen, the cook was hard at work on the royal breakfast. Busy as she was, she took a minute to check on the girl in the pantry, only to find her gone. What could have happened to her?

Two minutes later, a server came back from the great hall, quite distracted. "The princess's doll has come to life," she announced to the cook. "And she would like some more chicken."

The cook rolled her eyes and sent the server away with a plate of chicken. *Well,* she thought, *that answers that.*

A few minutes later, the pageboy came in the kitchen door from outside. He looked worried as he gave his boots a stamp, and asked her if she knew where he might find the king's manservant. She suggested he look in the king's chambers upstairs, and off he went.

The next thing the cook knew, the manservant himself came flying into the kitchen. He went straight to the pantry and looked around. He came out shaking his head. "I knew it!" he exclaimed.

"And what is it you know?" asked the cook.

"Well," said the manservant. "We've all been tricked. The pageboy just came back from the dollmaker's just now. He found a burnt up doll right by her fireplace. She begged the pageboy not to tell anyone. She said she was up all night working on new arms and head and all the rest of it. She won't be done for a week!"

Oh, no! thought the cook. *He knows about the dollmaker's girl!*

But the manservant continued. "Remember how heavy that doll was last night? That was no doll. That was a girl. And now," he said, pointing toward the great hall, "they think it's a doll come to life!"

"Yes, they do," affirmed the cook.

"Ah," said the manservant, tapping his head. "But I know better. They couldn't find the princess this morning. They still haven't found her."

"That is true," said the cook.

The manservant puffed out his chest. "Then there is no mystery, is there? There is no doll, only a burnt up thing. But there is a princess and somehow the dollmaker got her into that box last night."

The cook stopped stirring her pudding. "What? But doesn't the girl out there eating breakfast have a wooden leg? How do you explain that?"

"Ooh, that's a terrible thing," said the man. "The nursemaid put a spell on the princess when she was fired last night. The king's sitting out there right now, white as a ghost. He knows what's going on." And with that, the manservant went tearing back out of the kitchen to resume his duties.

The cook scratched her head. She gave a little laugh and looked at the rag box. Then she threw up her hands and went back to stirring her pudding.

Over the next week, the king lived in a state of complete confusion. He was afraid to be near his daughter, thinking he'd caused all this. But he was more afraid to leave her alone. What if the other leg should turn to wood? He was no longer sure how she should dress and told her maids not to braid her hair so tight. But when she appeared with little hairs sticking out everywhere, he worried that people would think he was neglecting her. He allowed all the toys from under the Christmas tree to be brought up to her room. Only now, just looking in the door made him feel ill, remembering how he had found her years ago, when he returned from the war. And he began to have nightmares.

The king's worry and confusion spread to other parts of his life. He began to forget things and he no longer spoke in a roar when something upset him. In his council chambers, he was frequently caught chewing on a thumbnail, staring off into space. He made decisions that made no sense to his councillors, like releasing people from the dungeon with no explanation, or having the number of torches in the castle doubled at night.

As for the dollmaker's girl, the cook worried she would miss her mother. So every day, she sent the kitchen boy to get news from the little house in the woods. Then, when she was done her duties for the evening, she would go up to the princess's room and sit with the poor girl for a while.

"Your mother was working on the arms today," she would say. Or, "She started to carve the feet this morning."

But the girl didn't care about any of that. She was worried because the servants wouldn't stop staring at her and she thought the king was crazy. "Am I supposed to be a doll or a girl?"

The cook shook her head. "Just play along. If the king thinks you're his daughter, be his daughter. If the servants think you're a doll come to life, be that. You'll be back home soon enough."

By the end of the week, the dollmaker had managed to carve and paint a new doll's head and body. On the eve of the new year, she delivered the new doll, wrapped in a nettle shirt, to the kitchen door of the castle. The manservant was away visiting his family at the time, so the cook took the delivery.

"You've done a fine job," said the cook. "You wait here and I'll fetch your girl."

She took the doll, still wrapped in its shirt, with her as she went up the back stairs to the princess's room.

When the cook crept in with the doll, the girl ran past her and nearly burst the door down in her hurry to see her mother again. "Wait! Wait!" called the cook, and she made the girl switch clothes with the doll. Then she sat the doll in the chair by the fireplace and raced after the girl, who was now halfway down the stairs.

After a quick and tearful embrace at the kitchen door, the mother and her girl hurried back to their house in the woods. They were so relieved their trick had not been discovered that they forgot to ask about payment for the princess's doll.

Later that evening, when one of the maids came into the princess's room, she glimpsed the doll in the chair and went about her work, thinking the doll was the princess. "I'm just going to turn down your sheets, milady," she said. When the princess didn't answer, the maid looked over at the girl. "Are you alright? Is that leg of yours bothering you?"

She noticed the girl now had two wooden legs poking out of her dress and her eyes went wide. Then she saw the two wooden arms. And the head was tipped to one side and staring, as if the eyes were painted on. Screaming at the top of her lungs, the maid flew from the room. Everyone within earshot came running, including the king.

"What on earth is the matter, woman?" the king demanded.

The maid pointed to the princess's room and blubbered, "It's…it's not just her leg now. It's both legs. And her arms, too!"

A cold shock went up the king's spine. *"Button by button, braid by braid,"* he remembered the old nursemaid saying. He turned around, took one trembling look into his daughter's room, and rushed down to the great hall, where he called for the captain of the guard.

"Find my old nursemaid. I don't care if she's a thousand miles away. Find her tonight!"

It was not difficult to find the old woman, who was back living in her own little house near the edge of the town. The captain brought her to the castle and offered her a chair in the great hall to wait. But she refused the chair and stood leaning on her cane.

As soon as the king was notified, he came storming down the stairs and began bellowing. "What do I need to do to bring my daughter back from this enchantment?" he demanded. "She has now become a doll. Both of her legs, her body, arms, and all."

The old nurse had no idea what he was talking about. The king had clearly lost his mind. But one thing she knew for certain: he was handing her tremendous power over him and she was not about to waste it. "This is not my doing," she said, "but yours."

"That does not help me get her back," he moaned.

The nurse stood up as straight as her old back would let her. "Let me be clear. You have spent all this time treating her like a doll, and she has become one. What do you think needs to be done now? What would a good father do?"

These words cut the king to the quick. He searched the old woman's face, not knowing what to say. Then he looked to the captain of the guard, who was waiting, and with a fierce growl and a brush of his hand, the king told him to take the old woman back to her home.

As if in a trance, the king slowly ascended the stairs. Finding it difficult to breathe, he went out on the balcony that overlooked the courtyard. As he stood there in the snow, he watched the gates being opened for his captain and the old woman, then closed again after them. And suddenly he felt completely alone. His harsh ways had pushed away the queen and now it was his girl's turn. How could he be the cause of this when his intentions were so good?

His eyes fixed on the faint light from a distant farmhouse window. It was like a small spark of warmth in the cold. He had a glimmer of what he must do, though the idea was still as dim as that small light in the distance.

The next day, the king had his entire schedule rearranged. His time in the council chambers was cut in half. Trips he had planned were cancelled and the large room at the front of the castle where he kept his trophies, his swords and armour, was cleared out and laid with beautiful carpets. All of the princess's toys were brought into the new room. The curtains were drawn and a big armchair was placed by the fire, which was kept roaring day and night. A large bolt was installed on the inside of the room, and the king ordered that he was never to be disturbed while he was in there.

Still, the servants wanted to know what was going on. That first day, the king carried the doll into the room and bolted the door behind him. Toward the end of the first week, they thought they could hear the king reading a story out loud, but perhaps he had gone mad and was muttering to himself. He always ordered tea and cakes with two cups and two plates. But no one was really sure what he was up to. All they knew was, the king would carry that painted doll into the room in the morning and bring it back out and put it to bed at night. The kitchen boy said he spied under the door one day and saw the big man on the floor with the doll, playing carts and horses, but no one believed him.

Three years passed and nothing changed within the walls of the castle. The guards guarded and the servants served. The king tried everything to reverse the enchantment. He made an effort to soften his voice and to speak kindly to everyone, even when there was good reason to be loud. He hired famous physicians from far countries to come and look at the doll. He banned face powder and made a law that no girl in the kingdom should have her hair braided too tight or have to wear stiff dresses. Finally, he thought to undo the magic by returning the girl's room to the way it was when he had come home from the war. He had toys scattered about the room, an old bare tree put up in one corner and clothes strewn here and there. He even broke a leg from the bed to show it was alright if she jumped on it. But nothing seemed to work.

In the little house in the woods, the dollmaker fell ill in the second year and died in the third. Her daughter tried to make the best of it, making dolls for the children in the town. This did not bring in much money, so she resorted to gathering firewood in the forest. But since there were grown men and women doing the same, she never sold enough to keep herself from starving.

Then one cold winter night near the third Christmas, she went begging around the town. She ended up at the kitchen door of the castle and the kindly cook took her in.

"I know you," she said. "I know you well. Come and warm yourself by the fire."

The girl and the cook began talking and at the end of it, the cook told the girl the whole story of who she was and how she had come to live at the dollmaker's house.

"So, now I'm a princess?" she asked.

"You always have been, girl. And all these years, your father has been waiting for you to return."

Needless to say, the king nearly lost his mind with happiness the day the doll turned back into a real girl. And he knew that all his care and learning to be gentle were well worth the effort. The cook had to hide the wooden doll. So for a second time, the dollmaker's work was burned up, this time in the cook's kitchen fireplace. No one was the wiser, and the ashes were thrown out the kitchen window with the turnip peelings.

The girl was glad to trade her rags for a fancy dress, her straw bed for a feather one. Though she was a bit old for some of the toys, she played with them anyway to please her father. Many people thought the king was crazy for spending so much time with her on the playroom floor. But she was to rule the kingdom one day, and if this was how he wanted to teach her royal ways, so be it. For even if her father was crazy, well, he was her father, after all.

As for the princess, she made a small living putting her pony to work, pulling carts and delivering messages. Just as she'd done when she was a little girl, she ate when she was hungry, slept where and when she liked, and dressed as she pleased. The one habit she couldn't shake was her hair, for she found she couldn't get to sleep unless it was in braids. And though she was afraid of wolves, she loved to make her bed outside, under the boughs of large trees. She worked her way north like this and eventually took up with a group of travellers who made toys and foul-smelling cures. These they sold to workers in the field, or to soldiers, if there happened to be a war.

The Brave Houseboy

The Brave Houseboy

There was once a boy who lived in a small house below the steep walls of the king's castle. The boy was the son of a sailor and he was told his father had died in a fierce storm, the likes of which had never been seen before or since. He was also told his mother had died of heartbreak when she heard the news. But if the truth were known, his father had been drunk in a foreign port and was served a plate of bad squab. He died spilling his guts into a wooden pail. And far from heartbreak, his mother slipped on her own skirts while she was yelling at a fishwife and took a deadly tumble down the harbour steps.

The boy was taken in by a wealthy sea captain to work as his houseboy. The boy's father had worked on the old man's ship and the captain felt he couldn't leave the child in the street to starve. But many a night, the boy thought living on the street might have been a better fate. For though the captain was rich and had a fine house and even a cook to make his meals, he ate like a sparrow and thought the rest of his household should do the same.

The cook, who was thin and sour, had little to do, since the captain ate the same thing every day. The cook's son had less to do, as his sole job was to bring the captain his dinner and wash his one plate afterward. Nevertheless, he called himself the captain's steward, though he was no more a steward than he was a pickerel, and he hated the houseboy from the moment he came to stay there.

The houseboy's job was to shake out the captain's bed, dust the books in his library, empty his chamber pot, and do everything that the cook and her son were too lazy to do. In payment for his work, the boy was given a corner to sleep in, a shirt that smelled like the old man, and a bowl of porridge every day.

The older boy teased and mistreated him whenever possible. Countless times, the houseboy spent the day sawing wood for the captain's fire, only to find the steward had thrown it all over the cliff into the sea. Or when they were eating at midday out back of the kitchen, the steward would spit in his food while he was trying to eat, just for the fun of watching his chin quiver, as that was the only meal he would have for the day.

It would be difficult to tell who caused the houseboy more suffering, the captain or his steward. But while the steward was plainly cruel, the captain was not. He was merely old and set in his simple ways. He spent his time in a comfortable chair reading, with his little dog on his lap or taking slow, ponderous walks in the vast forest up behind the house. Books of every type lined his library walls, and a spyglass on a tall stand near the window allowed him to watch approaching ships and look at the moon and stars at night.

In his travels, the captain had visited many strange places and brought a wealth of curiosities home from afar. On the walls were rich tapestries, the heads of strange creatures, and—dear to the boy's heart—weapons. Often he would get lost in thought while standing on a chair, polishing the swords, maces and axes. Sometimes he would dream of being a hero as he dusted the bows and whistling arrows that hung there.

But of all the strange and beautiful things in the house that set the boy's imagination afire, there was one that was set apart and forbidden for him to touch. It was a horn of some great animal, with a simple brass ring around one end. It sat high on a shelf in a specially made cradle. The boy was never told its history or why the old man prized such an oddity. But over time, he came to learn its history.

The captain had a friend who would visit a few times a year, and always on New Year's Eve. He used to be the captain's first mate, but was now a ship owner himself. He had a short brown beard and a cap that never left his head. The two would sit up in the library, each with a tankard of ale, and recount their adventures. As the cook and her son couldn't be bothered to serve the captain after dark, it was the houseboy's job to refill their tankards till all hours of the night.

Every year, the boy heard another piece of the tale of the great horn. The first mate never failed to shake his head or give a hearty laugh whenever the subject came up. But the captain took the story very seriously, and had his friend make him a solemn promise over it. Always, toward the end of the night, when the last drinks had been drunk and the fire had quieted to embers, the captain's voice would become low and he would deliver the same directions using exactly the same words.

"On the evening of the day after I die, you must take this horn down from its cradle. Stand in the window and look to the place the sun has gone down over the sea. Then sound the horn with all your might. A man will soon come, asking for what is his. You must bring him into the woods behind the house and find a small brown thread poking from the ground. Show him the thread and say, 'Fair is fair and time is told' and he will answer, 'Each to each a life of gold.' Do this, and all my life's work will be done."

Every year, these words chilled the boy to the tips of his hair. And every year it was the same. The mate would clap his hand on the captain's shoulder, smile and make his promise. "Gladly," he would say. "Though I hate to see you gone to keep my word."

Year after year, the promise over the horn would fire the boy with curiosity. He would lie awake at night, wondering what it could all mean. Who was the man he spoke of? And what secret lay up in the woods behind the house?

Then one New Year's Eve, the old shipmates fell into talking about that one voyage, the one where the captain ended up returning with the great horn. The boy refilled their tankards more often than usual, wanting a reason to stay close to hear what they were saying. And it was then, with the jaws of the two men loosened, that all the parts of the tale fell into place.

When the captain was a young man, "with more brawn than brains," as he said, he went to sea to make his fortune. By hard work and after many years, he was able to buy his own ship and go where he wished. He knew he could never find riches along the common shipping routes, where there were already too many traders. So the young captain made it his business to travel to strange places, hoping to bring back goods no one had ever seen.

On one such trip, he came upon a large island where a giant was always attacking the emperor's castle and eating his sheep, his cows, and anything else he could get his great hands on. The giant had been doing this for many hundreds of years, back before the emperor's great-great-grandfather's time. And as the giant was still young, he was expected to continue for a thousand years or more.

The emperor had tried to get rid of the giant in every way possible, using the strength of every man on the island, the cunning tactics of every wise general in his army, and the power of every weapon in the kingdom. But after so many years, nothing had stopped the giant from destroying his people's livelihoods. So, desperate beyond desperation, the emperor offered a huge reward, a thousand thousand pounds of gold, to anyone who could rid the island of this destructive giant.

When the sea captain arrived on his ship, wanting to trade with the kingdom, the emperor was very rude toward him and his men. He kept them waiting for days in a filthy room for no reason. Then, when the emperor finally did see them, he treated them like thieves and had his guards follow them everywhere, swords drawn, making sure they paid double or triple price for everything they wanted. When their trade was done, they all laughed about it, but the captain never forgot.

Before he left the island, he said, the captain thought he would try for the gold. He told his crew they should make the ship ready to carry their precious cargo home, for he was sure he would win the prize.

Ten of the emperor's most trusted guardsmen and ten of the captain's sailors followed him into the hills of the island, where the giant lived. They travelled for seven days and when they arrived and began to make camp, the captain said, "No need for that, as we will be leaving within the hour."

The ten men of the king's guard and the ten crewmen from the captain's ship began to buckle their swords and sharpen their axes.

"No need for that," said the captain. "There will be no fighting."

They all started to follow him up the biggest hill, where the giant lived. But the captain stopped them. "No need for you to come," he said. "I can do this alone."

So the captain went up the hill while the ten soldiers and the ten sailors sat around scratching their heads, wondering what the captain was going to do. One of the sailors was overcome by curiosity. He followed him up the hill and hid while the captain approached the giant. Though he saw everything that went on between the giant and the sea captain, he was no wiser at the end of it.

The captain put his hands on his hips and called up to the giant, saying that he had something important to ask him, something that would please the giant greatly. Eventually the giant began wondering what this bold little man wanted. He bent his head low and the captain stepped onto his great earring and whispered something that the sailor couldn't hear. When the captain was done, he jumped back down and the giant sat up.

"Agreed," said the giant.

And the captain said, "I have ten of the king's guard and ten of my own sailors down the hill. Could you please tell them, and our deal is made."

So the giant leaned over the hill and bellowed, "By the hair of my chin, I swear not to eat the king's sheep or the king's cows or bother the king ever again."

The ten soldiers heard it and the ten sailors heard it, but to a man, they could hardly believe their ears. The giant then gave the captain a great horn with a brass ring at one end—no one knew why. They returned to the king's castle after seven days and the king had to believe the word of his ten best men. He gave the captain the thousand thousand pounds of gold and the captain sailed away, with no one knowing what he had said to the giant.

When the story was done, the captain's friend shook his head. "I will never forget the look on that king's face," he said. "I never saw a jaw drop so far. But it has been forty years and not one soul knows what you said to that giant."

The captain sat back in his chair and gave the first mate a long look. "Well, truth be told, I'm getting old and I hate to take it with me to the grave. Someone should have a laugh besides me."

"Finally," said the first mate.

"You're not to tell a soul," said the captain. "Agree to that and you can have the truth."

The first mate held up a hand. "Of course, I agree."

The captain sent the boy out and he pretended to go down the hall, but he crept right back to listen.

"At the time," said the captain, "I was afraid that if the emperor knew the wording of my bargain with the giant, he would have been so angry that he might have sunk our ship and probably had me killed."

"I didn't like him from the beginning, treating us so badly," grumbled the first mate. "But what about the giant?"

The old captain smiled. "Well, a man like me might live to be a hundred, but that giant, I heard, could live to be ten times that. I have always been a man of modest needs. I could never be bothered to spend a thousand thousand pounds of gold. It's just too much trouble. So I told the giant, 'I will have the gold for my lifetime. And when I die, you can have it for the whole of your lifetime.' He saw that I was an honourable man. He saw that I hadn't come up the hill with an army. And also, he hated that emperor more than I did, and was glad to trick him out of all his gold. So he agreed. He gave me this great horn to call him when my day was done, and that was an end to it."

The captain's mate just sat there and laughed quietly, shaking his head. "Forty years, I waited for that. Well, you're right, it was worth a good laugh." And they drank up their ale and of course, the mate gave his promise for another year.

From that day on, the boy looked up at the great horn in the library with a new sense of wonder. He would fall asleep thinking about the day when the giant would arrive to collect his gold. And when he was working in the forest, he couldn't help but look for some sign of the small brown thread, for surely that was where the gold was buried.

Otherwise, life carried on just the same in the captain's household for many months. In the mornings, the captain could usually be found reading in his library. And after a meagre meal at midday, he would go for his walk. Sometimes he would bring his spyglass out into the yard to see what the ships were unloading. Or, when he was bored with that, he'd watch the people of the town or the king's guards walking the battlements.

To avoid the steward, the boy learned to bring his cut wood in when the captain was there to see it. But that didn't stop the steward from pinching him or giving him a kick at every opportunity. He once tried to stand up to the steward, though that ended up with him knocked to the floor and being slapped till he spat blood.

As much as things stayed the same inside the walls of the captain's house, things outside, in the rest of the kingdom, were about to change forever. Beginning in the third year of the houseboy's service to the old captain, people began talking about war and battles and whether their kingdom was safe. Other countries nearby had been invaded by horsemen from the east they called Tartars, who overran the villages and castles and stole everything. Most times, the first thing they did was kill the king and make his army their own.

Almost a year passed with near constant rumours about the invaders. Then one day, messengers arrived saying the Tartar army was on the move. It was expected to arrive in one month.

The steward taunted the houseboy with stories he made up about the Tartars. "They use runts like you for target practice. Then they boil your bones for soup."

But the cook was genuinely afraid. "There's no hope for the likes of us," she'd mutter into her cooking pot. "If we had brains or money we'd be off in the first ship that sailed."

The month was full of furious preparations. The king was a young man of no more than twenty years, but he was determined to save his kingdom. Every ironsmith and bow maker in the land was pressed into the king's service. And whatever stocks of grain and animals could be spared were brought into the castle in case there was a long siege.

When the Tartars finally arrived, they mustered in the fields to the east for nearly a week. They had twice as many horses as men and every man and every horse was small and swift. The whole castle flew into a panic; everyone rushed about, blocking doors and wetting down their thatched roofs in case the Tartars tried to set fire to them.

On the morning of the seventh day, the Tartars stormed the castle. Most of the soldiers and their families were murdered in their houses, and when they caught him, they tied the king up as if he were a pig for market and threw him from a high cliff into the sea.

All afternoon townsfolk fleeing the battle stopped at the captain's house on their way to distant places. Late in the day, as the smoke from the town's fires hung like a canopy over the cove, three men of the Tartar army, drunk and reckless, rode up the winding path from the town and tried to break in the captain's door. But the captain was there with three big men from the town, all of them armed.

The boy heard the struggle downstairs, heard the clash of swords and the sudden, final sound of the captain's great axe. He watched from the library window as one of the Tartars ran off and the old man and his friends took the bodies of the other two to the edge of the cliff and pushed them off.

The old captain was wounded that day, a place high on his chest pierced by the Tartar's curved sword. The cook patched it with cloth from an old shirt and some dried leaves from a musty bottle. He told her it felt better, though plainly it was not.

Over the next several days, people fleeing the Tartars kept arriving at the house, hoping for food, money, or refuge. All of them brought news, but no one had any that was good.

"They are trying to take all the men to work for them," one of them said. "They say there will be peace if we don't fight back."

"There'll be no one left to fight," said another, "if they keep throwing people into the sea."

It was only a matter of days before the stores amassed in the castle were all gone into the greedy bellies of the Tartar army. They raced to the harbour when a boat came in and stripped it clean of all its fish. The same happened when a farmer tried to sell his meat or vegetables in the town. They told him he was lucky to escape with his life, and should be proud to be feeding his new masters.

With everything being stolen by the invaders, soon there were no boats or ships arriving in port, no fishermen going out to fish, and no farmer from the countryside daring to come to market. But the Tartars stayed on. And at week's end, the wives and children of the Tartars arrived and moved into the lavish suites in the castle.

The boy was kept close to the house. The captain allowed him to go outside only to empty chamber pots or to bring in firewood. The captain's wound, despite all the treatments and dressings the cook applied, seemed to affect his arm. As he sat for long hours reading with his little dog on his lap, his arm hung limp as a dead thing by his side. The captain's hair and beard had always been shot through with white and grey. Now it shocked the boy to see how pure white they had become and how deep-set the lines were beside his eyes. Many a day the little dog would perk up in his lap and whimper, then lick the old man's face as if to assure himself that it was sleep that cradled his master, and not death.

Ten days after the Tartars arrived, as the season's first snows began to fly past the windows, a messenger from the Tartar king arrived on the captain's doorstep.

"Should I let him in?" asked the steward. "He's holding out a knife with jewels on it."

"Perhaps it's a gift," said the captain. "Let him in to say his piece."

The messenger stepped sheepishly inside and stood before the captain. He bowed low, and said, "The king is your humble servant and begs your kindness and mercy. He sincerely apologizes for the drunken soldiers who attacked your house. It was not his intention to harm or offend the captain." The messenger then presented the jeweled knife, laid across his two hands. When the captain accepted it from him, he continued. "The king, your humble servant, would be honoured if you would grace his halls and break bread with him in two days' time. To discuss a lasting peace," he added.

When the captain agreed to the meeting, the messenger backed away, greatly relieved, and hurried away to the castle.

News that the captain was going to meet with the Tartar king spread quickly. People wondered what the king wanted. Was it just a trick? Why was he being so nice to the captain? But whatever the reason, whatever the Tartar king had planned, the old captain never lived to attend the meeting.

Four townsfolk were killed by the Tartars the next morning for stealing grain from the army's supply. Then their families, down to the smallest babe, were locked in the castle dungeon. When the captain heard this, he rose from his chair, though he was barely able to do so. He paced for a while, holding onto the table and the walls for support until he had to sit down again. Then he wrote several messages and sent the steward off to deliver them.

Throughout the day, men arrived from the countryside to decide what to do. Others came to volunteer for a rebellion against the invaders. They would build an army, they said. Farmers, fishermen, boys and old men, they would join together to fight the Tartars and drive them from the castle. The captain stayed up all night with them, working out details of the rebellion. But he was so unwell, he took his ale by the spoonful and coughed up more than he took in.

The houseboy overheard the cook telling her son, "Get in there and take the old captain his drink. Maybe he'll give you something nice before he dies."

By morning, with the house nearly full, the captain was too ill even to leave his chair by the fire. And still people came, people offering themselves, their sons, or their money to help fight the Tartar king. Some had remedies for the old man's cough, others came just to hear the news or voice their anger. Women and children were being imprisoned! they raged. Their neighbours were starving! But as the house bustled with planning and the noise of bitter voices, the captain fell asleep in his favourite chair, his hand resting on his little dog. And when they went to wake him, they found he had died there in his sleep.

So the house full of anger and secret planning turned to a house of mourning. One of the farm wives found a length of sailcloth and they wrapped the captain in it and laid him out on the table on the main floor. Men went out with shovels and began poking the ground to find a soft place for a grave. The houseboy and the steward were told to go around and collect stones and heap them near where the captain would be buried.

Morning quickly turned to afternoon and news of the captain's death leapt from house to house. People came from near and far to pay their respects. They brought food they had managed to hide from the Tartars and dabbed their eyes, nodding and whispering to each other in the kitchen. Though the boy was surrounded by what seemed an endless stream of kind and neighbourly people, no one spoke to him, as he wasn't a friend or a relative. He tried to pet and cheer up the little dog. It had curled up under the table, sighing deeply now and again and ignoring its food and water. No matter what he did, the little dog refused to leave the spot.

Just as the sun began pouring in the west windows of the library, there came a loud knock at the door, a very unfriendly knock, and immediately the boy remembered the great horn that stood in its cradle on the shelf.

At the door were two wiry Tartars who pushed their way in and declared they had come to take the death tax their king was due. No one knew what they were talking about. They gruffly explained that by their law, their king was due part of the property of any man who died under his rule, and they had come to collect it. They quickly overcame the men who tried to force them from the house and went upstairs, straight to the shelf where the great horn sat.

"Only this," said one of them as they pulled it from its cradle. And the Tartar soldiers left the house and were gone.

The houseboy stood speechless, having forgotten how to breathe, white as the captain's sailcloth. No one paid him any attention. They were all counting themselves lucky that only the horn was taken, and not their lives. But the captain's words rang in the boy's ears: *"Do this, and all my life's work will be done."* The tragedy of it crushed him. How could this happen? Where was the first mate?

Evening turned to night and the visitors slowly left to go home. The cook and her son, knowing their days in the captain's house were numbered, heaped the fireplace with wood, not caring that they were wasting it. The boy went to his bed upstairs and the captain's little dog followed and nestled into the crook of his arm.

Now that the captain was gone, he wondered what would become of him. He had no living relation, no money or skills that would bring him work. Perhaps he could work for the Tartars in the castle. At least he'd be fed there. He heaved a frustrated sigh, knowing he'd be thought of as a traitor. But which was worse, he asked himself, being hung as a traitor or slowly freezing out in the snow?

With these dark thoughts, he rolled over and curled himself around the little dog. He could feel its warm breath under his ragged blanket and he found it comforting. Just as he began to drift off to sleep, he heard a strange, hollow sound from outside. He had opened the window above him a crack because of the heat from downstairs and the sound came in on a ribbon of chill air. It was a long, low sound, like a moaning ghost or an animal. He knew immediately what it was and it made his heart sink in his chest. It was the horn, sounding at the lips of a Tartar at the top of the castle wall.

The boy could not have said how long the horn sounded. The captain's little dog didn't know whether to stand up on the bed and confront it, or back away in fear. But the sound eventually stopped, far into the night. Toward morning, in his distress, his mind drifted in and out of horrid dreams, with the dog trembling beside him.

Eventually the sun crept over the eastern horizon and found the boy sitting on his bed, staring into the dim corners of the room, shivering. There were no strange sounds from outside, just the quiet roar of the distant waves and the occasional seabird. And there were no sounds at all from downstairs in the house that should have made the little dog look up suddenly and bark. But the dog had sensed something that brought him to his feet and made his fur bristle.

When the little thing backed away down the bed, away from the open window, the boy stood and looked outside. But squint and rub his eyes as he might, he could see nothing amiss. By now the dog was going mad in the room, barking and whimpering. The boy pulled his blanket over his shoulders and hurried to the library where the spyglass stood, the dog following. Even when the boy put it to his eye and looked out across and beyond the cove, he could see nothing. The dog continued to bark and ran anxious circles around his legs.

Then he trained the spyglass on the distant place where the sea met the sky, and he saw something that made him look away and rub his eyes. When he looked again he was sure it was no illusion, and this time jumped back in shock. For the spyglass showed, on the farthest horizon, the head and shoulders of a man rising out of the water. And no ordinary man, for in the time it took for the boy to move his eye from the spyglass and squint into the distance, the man was bigger than he had been in the spyglass, so fast was he approaching. The little dog was now so excited he was knocking books from the library shelves and jumping up and down from the captain's favourite chair.

"You stay here," said the boy, looping a cord through the dog's collar and tying the other end to a desk leg. And out of the library and down the stairs he ran. He flung open the house door and dashed across the yard to the edge of the cliff.

The man was now waist deep in the water and twice the height of the high rock bluffs that curved around the cove. The motion of his great legs made waves crash on the beach and sprayed water over land that was never wet, even from the highest waves in the worst storms. The giant reached down, plucked two of the largest fishing vessels from the water, and set them on the far cliff, out of harm's way. And still he strode on, till his boots kicked water up the beach so far that it arched right over the town and splashed the castle walls.

The gruff voices of shouting men and the cries of women drifted up the hill. People were fleeing the town, some up the hillside, others into the open gates of the castle, the walls of which were now lined with Tartar soldiers.

The giant stood at the water's edge for some time, surveying the scene below him. Someone on the castle's battlements briefly sounded the horn again and the giant looked to see where it was coming from. Then, with a motion that knocked every book from its shelf and every plate from its cupboard for twenty miles around, the giant went to his knees on the beach. He braced his fingertips against the main street of the town and leaned close to the castle. His wet clothing dripped torrents of water onto the town.

The cook and the steward came flying out of the house to see the sight. Dumbfounded, they walked to the cliff edge where the houseboy stood, shading their eyes and squinting across the cove.

"Will you look at that!" said the cook.

"He's so huge!" her son exclaimed.

"And here we thought the Tartars were bad enough."

The giant seemed to be listening to someone on the castle wall. The boy couldn't see who it was from this distance. All he could tell was that they were holding up something to show the giant. Was it the horn? The giant crouched there, listening for some minutes, but from here all the boy heard were the cries of frightened townspeople and disturbed seabirds, and the crashing of the waves on the beach.

"What's he doing?" asked the steward.

The houseboy half wondered if he should run back to the house and get the spyglass so he could see better. But he did not need the spyglass to see what happened next.

The giant stood to his full height and surveyed the countryside around the town. His eye seemed to fix on something in the distance and with two steps, he was well over the town and castle and into the hills beyond.

The steward suddenly pushed the houseboy to the ground. "I can't see!" he yelled at him, though there was no more than the twig of a bush in his way.

"Hisht!" his mother barked at him, shading her eyes.

The houseboy got to his feet and saw the giant reach down and seem to sweep something together into a pile with his hands. And in another moment, he was back on the beach and laying a crushed mass at the foot of the castle.

"What is it?" asked the cook's son.

The cook's eyes narrowed even more. Then they shot open, so wide that the whites showed all around. She opened her mouth to speak, but no words came out.

Even from here, the houseboy could see what it was. There, at the foot of the castle, was a crushed mass of hundreds of men, their bodies poking from the trees and soil the giant had scooped from the ground.

"It's the farmers and…menfolk…" she began.

"What do you mean?" asked her son.

"It is our army," said the cook, clearly overwhelmed. "He's killed them all."

The following day, the captain's friends and neighbours came to bury him in the yard. But the kind words they spoke over his grave were barely heard. For behind them, the giant stood guard before the castle, his great arms folded on his chest, his eyes gazing at the western sky. And every time the giant twitched a whisker, people's heads jerked around in fear.

The boy finally discovered what had happened to the captain's first mate. He had gone out fishing and, knowing the Tartars were going to take it all, he poisoned the catch before he returned to port. The fish had killed thirty Tartar soldiers and sickened a hundred more before the man was caught. They killed him, the boy heard, on the night before the captain's passing. Remembering all the hours they'd spent drinking and talking as old friends, the boy found it terribly sad that neither the captain nor his first mate had been able to mourn the other's death.

After the captain was put in the ground and everyone came inside to warm themselves, the boy listened carefully for news and lingered to stoke the fire when something sounded interesting.

There was little talk of forming another army. Many of them wondered if they all shouldn't try to get a boat and flee the kingdom. "The Tartars don't know anything about sailing," a woman said, "so they won't be chasing us down."

"But where would we go?" someone asked.

"What does it matter?" said a young man with a bit of hair on his chin. "In two steps the giant can just pluck our whole boat out of the water and crush it."

But what made the boy perk up his ears the most was news brought by a servant from the castle. The wiry little man had managed to escape the Tartars the night before. When he spoke, he moved his hands constantly. "That Tartar king knew about the captain and that great horn. He knew it would bring that giant. But that's all he knew. Now that the giant's here, they don't know what to do with him. He's eaten nearly every goat and every cow in the kingdom. Ha! They are all worried about what to feed him next!"

The boy was glad to see all the neighbours and friends of the captain at the house. He was aware that some of them had only come to gawk or because there was free food. But what happened next made him question whether any of them cared about the captain at all.

No one knew what would become of the captain's house, his library, or all the beautiful things he had collected on his voyages. The law of the land had been pitched over the cliff with the king and no one wanted the Tartars to have any of it. So they decided, out of both goodness and greed, to strip the house of all the captain's fine things and hide them at their own houses. Over the course of the afternoon, with the little dog barking at everyone who came and went, people took away the contents of the house by the cartload. By dark, the library was bare to the walls. The downstairs was stripped of its tapestries and all that was left of the weapons were the pegs where they'd hung. They even took the cook's best pots and the boy's shabby blanket so that he spent the night not only shivering, but wondering how he would keep himself alive the next day, for there was hardly a cup of grain left in the kitchen.

But worse was to come. The following morning he was wakened with a kick from the steward. "Get out there and cut some kindling, you lazy thing. The fire's gone out again, no thanks to you." He had been kicked awake before, but this time it was so swift and hateful, it made his head swim and left a deep red mark on his cheek. The steward rolled him down the stairs and the cook was there, shouting for him to hurry up, as she wanted to make the last bit of porridge before they left the house forever.

As bad things come in bunches, they never got to eat a bite of their porridge. For two minutes after the water was boiling on the fire, the dog began barking at something outside and the houseboy saw people passing by the windows. And when the strangers pressed their faces to the windows to try to see in, he saw they were Tartars.

If the houseboy's life were a meal where he served others but was never fed himself, so began a new course. The Tartars moved into the captain's house and made it their own. There were four of them and a guard who slept across the door at night so no one could open it. The leader seemed to be some sort of commander in the Tartar army. He brought his wife, who was short and nearly bald, and his two grown daughters, both of whom had huge brown teeth that were twisted like the roots of a tree.

Over the next several days, the cook settled back into cooking, her son into serving, and the houseboy into providing wood for the fire. Only now, each of them had to work harder than they ever had for the sea captain. The cook was taught to make their strange bread and to cook meat in the Tartar way. They had brought strange spices, which made the cook sneeze and complain, "I can't take it. The whole house smells like a cow died in a pepper-corn fire." The steward spent half his days carrying water and standing like a statue next to the commander, waiting for him or his guard to need something. When winter arrived and the house grew cold, the boy was constantly in the forest, cutting, dragging, sawing, and splitting wood for the commander's fire.

And still the giant stood before the castle, arms crossed, either not noticing or not caring about the snow that draped his shoulders. The boy soon realized that he was the only person left alive who knew what the giant had come for. He considered searching the vast forest for the small brown thread that the captain had spoken of. But what if he found it? What then? He was more afraid of the giant than he was of the Tartars. Grown men had already died when the giant turned suddenly and they were crushed under a huge boot. He was right to be afraid and stay as far away from the giant as possible.

Then something unexpected changed his mind.

One morning he was awakened by a great tumult in the distance, deep growls that could only come from the giant and shouts of anger and anguish from the Tartars. The boy got up and opened the window that faced the castle. The giant had crouched to lean over the battlements into the courtyard. He wondered what the Tartars were yelling about, for the giant seemed to be ignoring them. Then he saw that the giant was plucking the Tartars' beloved horses from the castle stables. When he got five or six in his great hand, he popped them into his mouth like cheese curds, then reached over for more. The Tartars, crowded all around the castle walls and even perched on the high turrets, were shouting like madmen for the giant to stop.

When their furious shouts did nothing, they began firing arrows and spears at the giant whenever he bent low. The giant completely ignored them, which made the Tartars even angrier. Then some cruel soldier had the idea of setting the arrows on fire before shooting them at the giant. At first the giant didn't notice, but then the legs of his trousers caught fire and his anger began to show. As he ducked his head to see what was wrong, an arrow with a rope caught his one great earring. And when twenty or thirty Tartars began to haul on it, the giant gave an anguished cry that echoed across the countryside.

As he watched the giant pat out the fires and heard him grunt in pain as he rubbed his ear, the boy realized someone needed to help the giant. And it was then that he decided to search in earnest for the small brown thread.

Up in the forest, the sea wind had blown the few remaining fall leaves over the thin layer of snow. Between the trees, everything that wasn't white was some shade of brown: the grass that poked up here and there, all the twigs and bracken and dry leaves above and below the snow. At first the enormity of his task discouraged the boy. How could he find one small thread in this vast place?

Whenever he could spare a moment, he searched off the main paths between the trees, kicking snow away and brushing with his wet and frozen sleeves. As evening came and he began tripping over snags in the dim light, he would return with his load of wood for the Tartar commander.

One morning, when the boy woke and went out to fetch his firewood and resume his search, the cook and her son were outside, jumping around and cheering.

"The giant's gone! Look! He's gone!" But their happiness was a bit too hasty.

Though the sky was clear, the boy heard what sounded like thunder in the eastern distance, and he imagined the giant was at work there, beyond the horizon. Sure enough, the giant soon returned to his place before the castle. He had his shirt stuffed full of large deer, which he ate by the handful, then picked his teeth with the antlers of the last one.

The boy spent the day again in the forest, cutting wood as quickly as possible so he would have time to search. He neatly piled the logs he had cut and hurried off to search for the thread. He thought he would try a new direction today, over a far hill where he rarely went. But by the time he got there, the sky had turned grey and it had begun to snow. His tracks were soon covered, one tree began to look like another, and he found himself lost for most of the afternoon. When he finally found his way out, it was quite dark. So, head down, shivering, and soaked to the skin, he returned to the house and was beaten by the Tartar guard for being so late while the steward watched and grinned.

The next day he didn't search at all, but cut as much wood as he could in order to please the Tartar. The day after that, the giant was gone again all morning, but soon returned with his shirt full of some fat seals with two great white tusks sticking down from their mouths. The giant ate them one at a time, for he seemed to like how they squished when he bit into them.

The boy went off to the forest to continue his search. He was now determined to find the small brown thread. He had decided to work in one little place, move every flake of snow and blade of grass, and mark the trees nearby to remind himself that he had been there. But by noon he had only worked a spot the breadth of his outstretched arms. He had to spend the rest of the day with his axe and saw or face another beating from the guard. How could he hope to find the thread this way? And what if he should miss it and have to backtrack and search again?

This went on until spring. Every day the boy would go out, move each leaf and snowflake and blade of brown grass till he'd cleared a small area, then chop firewood for the Tartars all afternoon. Some mornings the boy would go out and find the giant with his shirt full of great gray whales, biting their heads off and wiping his greasy lips on his sleeve. Other days, after a heavy meal, the giant would step up to the far cliff and have a sleep. He'd make strange snoring noises, great rumbling snorks that rattled all the windows in the town. Sometimes he would be so deeply asleep, he would roll over and fall off the cliff into the sea. Startled awake, he would get up and kill Tartars when he heard them laughing from the battlements, flicking them across the countryside like bits of earwax.

Then one morning, the houseboy was out in the forest with the captain's little dog. The dog usually stayed with the Tartar girls, but this morning their father got up and stepped in the mess the dog had left outside his room during the night. The commander threatened to kill it, but his daughters cried and pleaded with him till he shouted at the boy to take the dog from his sight, out into the forest with him for the day.

In the many months he had been searching the forest floor, the boy had only worked a small area, as far across as he could throw a stone. Today, as he pawed the thawing ground, sick in his heart that the new grass was coming in and making his work twice as hard, he had a terrible feeling he had already missed the thread. He still had years of forest to search and the area he had already done seemed hardly worth the trouble. Then he spotted the little dog digging furiously at a patch of ground a short distance from him. *Is he just copying me?* the boy wondered. Was there just some old bone buried there?

When he went over to see what the dog was digging for, he saw nothing at first. The trees here were all shorter than those nearby, and the ground seemed to be somewhat softer. He began helping the dog push away the roots and the soil. The dog went away sniffing every once in a while, but he always came back to the same spot.

The two dug and explored for the next ten minutes. About to give up, the boy sat back and looked at the mess of soil and grass and roots they had made. And there, poking up, was a very thin, braided thread no longer than his small toe. He got a twig and loosened the soil around it. And then a piece of branch so he could shovel at the hard ground. The thread got thicker the deeper he dug; soon it was as fat as his little finger. And still he dug. He dug until he had a hole around the cord so deep he could only touch the bottom with his fingertips. He tried pulling on the cord, but it wouldn't move.

The boy sat back on his haunches and wiped the happiness from his eyes. "I don't know why I'm so glad," he said to the little dog. "We have what the giant came here for, but now we have to tell him where it is."

But whatever fears or happiness the boy had at that moment was suddenly swept away. Someone grabbed his hair from behind, dragged him backward, and knocked his head against the nearest tree. In his struggle to escape, he saw it was the steward, who put his foot onto the boy's throat.

"So," he said, "this is what you've been looking for all these months. Now I'll be the hero, if you please." Then he kicked and dragged the boy far into the forest, where he beat him till he knocked him senseless. He used the houseboy's rope belt and the leather strings from his shoes to tie him to a tree by the neck and wrists. He picked up the little dog and carried it snarling and yipping under his arm, back to the house.

The steward dropped the dog inside and even though the guard ordered him back, he ran as fast as he could down the cliffside path toward the town and the giant standing before the castle. He told the first Tartar soldier he met that he had a means to rid the kingdom of the giant. When the soldier asked him to prove it, the steward said, "I serve in the house where the great horn came from. And now I know its secret."

The soldier brought him under the legs of the giant into the castle. He was taken before the Tartar king and the king waved them away, saying, "Let him say what he wants to the giant. If he's wrong, the giant will kill him."

So the steward was led through the courtyard and up onto the battlements. He called and called, but the giant either did not hear him or was deliberately ignoring him. The soldier went down into the castle and returned with the great horn. He sounded it with a spluttering honk and finally the giant turned and looked down at the miniscule steward.

"I know the secret of the great horn and what you have come here for!"

The giant blinked and seemed interested.

The steward continued. "The horn belonged to a sea captain, but he is now dead. The king here took the horn as a death tax. I served in the captain's house."

The moment he said this, the giant spun around. "Where is this house?" he thundered.

The steward pointed over the town to the stone house on the cliff overlooking the cove. The next moment, he hardly knew what was happening, it happened so fast. The giant's great brown hand came toward him and grabbed a chunk of the stone battlement with him and the soldier all mixed up with the heavy stones. The giant plucked the horn from the mess, threw the soldier away, and put the horn in his shirt pocket. Then he strode over the town and the cove. Standing in the water below the cliff, the giant dropped the steward and the chunks of wall onto the grass before the house.

"Show me," he growled.

The steward staggered to his feet. As the Tartars came out of the house with the little dog following them, barking madly, the steward hurried up into the forest. Without moving, the giant watched him scurry away under the leafless canopy. When the steward got to the place where the boy had been digging, the giant took one step, cracking trees under his feet, and stood over the spot to look down at the tiny bit of disturbed ground.

"There you are," said the steward, pointing out the spot to the giant.

The giant bent down, peered at the dug up dirt, then looked at the steward. Expecting the giant to start digging, the steward leapt out of the way. But the giant did nothing of the kind. He stood to his full height again, folded his arms over his chest, and remained there, no matter what the steward said or did.

For the next three hours, the giant did not move. The Tartar guard came from the house to see what was happening, then half the town and castle arrived. They encircled the spot where the brown thread protruded and some tried digging deeper and others tried pulling it from the ground. They questioned the steward, who knew nothing further, and shouted up at the giant, asking what he would like them to do. But the great arms stayed folded and the giant did not move or speak.

Off in the woods, where there was still hard-packed snow in the shadows, a chill was creeping into the boy's bones from the cold ground. He saw some townspeople cutting through the forest on their way to see the giant and called out to them, "Help, please! Can you help me?" But they were too far away and the only one who heard him was the steward, who came back to whip him with a switch and tell him to be quiet.

When the steward ran back to where the giant was standing, the commander's guard caught him by the collar. "Have you seen the houseboy? The commander's fire needs fuel and he's nowhere to be found."

The steward shrugged and said, "No, I haven't seen him."

The giant had watched the steward go off into the forest, and seen and heard all he'd done, but he remained silent.

Soon the houseboy's neck and wrists were turning blue where they were tied. Seeing some Tartar soldiers coming toward him, he called out to them. "Help! Hey, please, can you help me?" But they laughed and pointed and walked right by. The only one who paid him any mind was the steward, who came back to whip him again with a switch and tell him to be quiet.

When the steward ran back to where the giant was standing, the commander himself was there. "Do you know where the houseboy is? The house is freezing."

The steward said, "No, I have no idea."

The giant's right eye twitched at this, but he said nothing.

By the third hour, hundreds of people had arrived to see the sight, having heard that the steward knew what the giant was waiting for. By then, the houseboy was fainting from the cold and knew he might die if someone didn't find him. So with no one to hear him he called out, "Please! Is there anyone near who can help me?" Again, the only one who heard him was the steward, who came back with his switch to whip him till he was quiet.

When the steward ran back to where the giant was standing, his mother the cook was there. "Have you seen that houseboy? The commander is going to want his supper and my fire needs wood."

Annoyed, the steward threw up his hands and snapped, "I don't know!"

The giant had again watched the steward cross the forest, and seen and heard everything. But this time he did not remain silent. He was tired of standing there waiting for the steward and the steward obviously had something to hide. He gave a deep growl and, with the gawkers all fleeing, strode across the forest to where the houseboy was bound to the tree. He took hold of the tree and with one light tug, pulled it from the ground. Then he snapped it so the boy could be free.

The houseboy lay on the ground as the townsfolk hurried over, wondering what the giant was doing. The boy got his hands free and took the rope from his neck. But he was nearly frozen and had been hurt when the giant broke the tree. He could see the steward rushing toward him, plainly intent on keeping him quiet. He knew what he had to do, but fear suddenly took hold of his throat.

Seeing the giant in the distance was one thing, but standing so far beneath him was quite another. He'd seen the giant crush hundreds of men at once, seen him eat huge creatures from the land and sea, and watched as he licked their fat and blood from his lips. He had never been so afraid in his life and for a long moment he did not know what to do to stop being afraid. Then just as the steward came within spitting distance, the boy saw the ragged hem of the giant's burnt trousers. He remembered how the giant had cried out when the Tartars were mean to him and all at once, he found his voice.

"Fair is fair," he called up to the giant as loudly as he could, "and time is told."

The giant had been standing there like some great dark wall. But when he heard these words, he bent to where the houseboy stood. "Each to each," he answered, "a life of gold."

The giant then gave a small smile and strode back to the place where the trees were shorter. He pushed the ground aside with one finger. When he was able to get a grip on the thread, he began pulling.

The boy limped through the woods. As he approached the dug-up area, the ground began heaving. Everyone watching had to hold onto trees or each other to stay upright. The giant now had two hands on the thread, which had thickened to a cord and then a thick sailor's rope. He let go a moment, spat on his hands, then gripped the rope and gave one great tug. A massive fishing net burst from the ground like a sack full of huge rocks.

The giant gave the net a shake and blew some of the soil from it and the rocks inside glinted in the sunlight. "A thousand thousand pounds of gold," said the giant with a great satisfied smile. He turned and took one stride back out of the forest, then stepped down into the sea. He began dipping and sloshing the net in the water to wash off the dirt.

Everyone had followed him—the boy, the townspeople, the Tartars. They all gathered at the edge of the cliff while the giant admired his treasure. From the town, more people were coming out to the beach or starting up the hill to watch the giant.

He set his net down in the water and strode across the cove and over the town to stand before the castle once more. "Bring me your king," the giant roared at the Tartars.

The king was already on the battlements. He stepped forward, chin raised in defiance. The giant reached down and picked up the Tartar king between his fingers. That was the last anyone saw of him, for when the giant was done rubbing his fingers together, there was nothing left but a small smear, which he wiped away on his pant leg. The next moment, every Tartar in the town and castle was picking up their heels and either running or riding back east, where they had come from.

Stepping back over the town and then the cove to retrieve his net from the water, the giant paused and looked at the boy who stood there in his pathetic shirt, its sleeves worn and filthy from his long search. Without a word, the giant reached into his net, took out a lump of gold about twice the size of the houseboy's head and dropped it in front of him. It broke into several pieces on the hard ground. Then the giant turned, slung the net over his shoulder and strode away through the water.

The boy's eyes went wide at the treasure lying before him. With this, he would never be hungry again, never lack for a roof over his head, and always have warm and comfortable clothes.

But this thought raced through his mind too soon. The moment the giant was in the distance, the steward and several quick and wiry Tartars came and grabbed the lumps of gold from the ground. The boy tried his best to stop them, to keep at least a few crumbs for himself, but to no avail. He fell to his knees on the ground, crushed at his loss, telling himself he was lucky to at least have his life.

The next moment, there came a great rushing sound from behind him. He stood and turned and saw the giant striding back toward him with a fierce look on his face, kicking a great froth of waves up the cliffs and into the cove. He stopped before the stone house once again and pointed sternly to everyone who had robbed the boy of his prize. Like children caught stealing, the Tartars and the steward all dropped the gold they had taken at the boy's feet and backed away, fearing the giant was going to crush them like the Tartar king. But he didn't.

Instead, the giant bent low to the houseboy and stared him straight in the eyes for a moment. Then he fished in his shirt pocket, brought out the great horn with the brass ring and laid it at the boy's feet. Pointing a huge finger at him, he said, "Fear nothing."

Then he rose to his full height again, slung the thousand thousand pounds of gold over his shoulder, and strode off into the sea, never to be heard from again.

So the houseboy took over the captain's house, as no one was about to argue that it should go to anyone else. The cook, it turned out, actually knew how to cook and porridge was never made in the house again. As for the steward, when the Tartars were finally all gone and the ships began bringing their cargo into port again, he thought he would seek his fortune at sea. But being forever lazy, he turned to piracy and was soon caught. He was punished by being tied into a net full of rock and sunk to the ocean's bottom.

The neighbours soon returned the treasures they had taken from the house and as time passed, the boy hired tutors so that he might learn to read all the books in the captain's beloved library. And there he would sit, with the little dog on his lap and later his own children, with his own story to tell of the weapons on the wall and the great horn upon the high shelf.

The Wishing Oak

The Wishing Oak

There was once a king who had two daughters and no wife as, some years ago, she had eaten too much cake and fallen off her shoes. The queen had been very tall, and thought if she could widen herself a bit she would seem normal sized. Sadly, she widened herself too much and when she fell off her shoes she could not get back up, and died.

Now, the king's eldest daughter was very odd. Her name was Princess Jamsine. Jamsine stayed in her room most of the day, trying on jewelry and dresses. When that made her tired, she would have a little lie-down, then perhaps she would get up long enough to try on a scarf. She never read books because when she tried to read them in bed, they would always drop on her face when she fell asleep. On the rare occasion when she did leave her room, she made sure she was fashionably late for everything, for she hated to be out of fashion.

The king's youngest daughter could not have been more different. Her name was Princess Ciminin and she seemed sensible from a very early age. She got out of bed when she was finished sleeping. She read books because she was curious and wore fancy dresses because they wouldn't let her go naked. People came to ask her questions, not because she always knew the answer, but because they liked her company. And even though she cared nothing for fashion, all the girls in the kingdom copied everything she wore. This was true even of her older sister.

From early on, Jamsine found it too much work to think for herself. When Ciminin accidently started a fashion, Jamsine immediately had her dressmakers copy it and told everyone it was her idea. Whenever Ciminin said something that sounded smart, Jamsine would repeat it to their father or one of his ministers, so that she sounded smart, too. After a while, people realized Jamsine was only leaving her room when she had a new dress or a fresh idea she had taken from her sister.

One day, when Jamsine was about ten years old, one of his ministers reminded the king that his eldest daughter was to be queen one day. "Being a queen is more than parading around in fine clothes," the minister said. "What if there is a war? It would be a terrible thing if the queen refused to get out of bed. And what if she can't find her little sister to ask her what to do?"

The king took his minister's worry to heart. He brought tutors and mentors and professors from the four corners of the kingdom, and made Jamsine study all the things she would need to know to be a good queen. But Jamsine arrived to her lessons fashionably late and usually left early because the lessons were too hard and she needed a little lie-down. After two years of this, the king finally threw his hands up and said, "Well, if she doesn't want to learn, all the tutors and mentors and professors in the world won't be able to help her." And he sent them all back to where they had come from.

Now, the king had things in common with each of his daughters. Like Jamsine, he preferred one room of the castle more than the others and rarely left it. That room was the library, where he spent his time reading, drinking endless cups of tea and playing with the jackdaw that nested by one of the library windows. But like Ciminin, the king was extraordinarily skilled at making people happy, especially his subjects. But since he rarely left the library or spoke to anyone, no one knew how he did it.

One of his subjects would need help one day and the next day some help would arrive. If someone fell ill, they might suddenly find some medicine or a doctor on their doorstep. If rats happened to eat all of a farmer's barley seed, a bushel basket of barley seed might appear on his windowsill the next day—even if he hadn't told a soul about his loss. Were there fairies that brought all the good things? Did the king have spies in every town and village? People suspected the king was the one responsible, but no one really knew for sure until the king fell ill. For it was then that fewer and fewer people were helped, no matter how much they needed it.

The king's health declined rapidly. It seemed that one day he was scrambling like a squirrel up the ladders in the library to fetch books from high shelves, and the next he was in his bed, barely able to catch a breath. Many days the king hardly had the strength to read or say a word to anyone, and would rest most of the time, a book lying open on his chest. Other days he would not wake at all, and talk in his sleep like a madman. "Where is John Smalls?" he would say. "The bird needs cheese, for the cobbler's hands are hurt."

"Does he mean the jackdaw by the library window?" asked Princess Ciminin. "And who is John Smalls?" But no one seemed to know who he was. Yet when she sent someone to inquire at the cobbler's, it was true that he'd hurt his hands and couldn't work to feed his children.

Another day, the king mumbled from his fevered dreams, "Where is John Smalls? The bird needs cheese, for the baker's boy is lost."

No matter who Ciminin asked, no one seemed to know who John Smalls was. And yet, it was true that the baker's boy was lost in the north woods.

On another day, the king moaned, still sound asleep, "Where is John Smalls? The bird needs cheese, for the alewife is ailing."

Princess Ciminin continued to ask about this John Smalls person. But no one had ever heard of him. And yet, when she sent someone to the alehouse, it was true that the alewife was very sick.

Not long after, the king died and the whole kingdom went into mourning. For the first time, Ciminin lost her smile and could barely say a word to anyone. Her sister Jamsine spent her days screaming at maids about which black dress to wear. She was tolerated because everyone knew she was trying not to think of her dead father or the fact that she would soon have to replace him in his duties.

People came from far and wide to see their much-loved ruler laid to rest. There was a grand funeral and procession with dozens of carriages pulled by large black horses and the entire castle guard following behind. No one was being helped now, which made everyone sure the king had been responsible.

The day after the king was buried, the court's high chancellor called all the king's ministers and all the king's family together to read the royal will. Everything in the reading of the will went along as people expected, except for two things. Someone named John Smalls was to be given a large bag of gold along with a note thanking him for his years of faithful service to the king. No one knew who John Smalls was, so they went to the next item in the will. It said: *Sadly, the king regrets to inform Princess Jamsine that, even though she is the eldest, she will not be the new ruler of the kingdom. It is the king's will that Princess Ciminin, on account of her good sense, shall become the Queen of All the Land and be crowned immediately.*

Though many had feared this might happen, it was still a great shock to everyone in the room. Only the eldest son or daughter had ever been named king or queen before this. Everyone understood why the king had made this decision, but understanding didn't help Princess Jamsine. All the blood drained from her face and she rushed from the room as if someone had just slapped her—which, in a way, they had.

The next day, Princess Ciminin was crowned Queen of All the Land. Her sister stood beside her, fuming throughout the ceremony, hating this very public humiliation, hating that it wasn't her being crowned. Secretly, she was happy that she would never have to do all the hard work that came with being queen. But that small happiness was far outweighed by the knowledge that she would never be the centre of attention again.

There was a huge banquet after the crowning of Queen Ciminin, with lively music and course upon course of rare and delicious dishes. But as people began to leave, one of the castle guardsmen approached the queen and said there was someone waiting to speak to her in the royal library.

"He is quite, um…an unusual gentleman," said the guard, "and he says it is very important."

Princess Jamsine overheard the guard and as the new queen excused herself and hurried to the library, Jamsine secretly followed her. Once Queen Ciminin entered the library, Jamsine tiptoed up and peered in through the crack between the library doors. There, she saw bowing before her sister a very tiny man, no more than knee high.

"My name is John Smalls," he said, his hat in his hand, "and I am here to help you."

"The king has left you a large bag of gold," said Ciminin. "But no one knew who you were."

"Who I am and what I do must remain a secret," said John Smalls. "As I served your father, I hope to serve you."

"And how would you do that?" asked the queen.

John Smalls asked Ciminin to bend down so he could speak softly to her, and Jamsine had to press her ear to the crack between the doors to hear him.

"There is a very old oak tree," said John Smalls, "in the dark wood to the north of the castle. People call it the wishing oak. For a hundred years people have trusted the oak to help them. If they are in dire need, they tell the tree their troubles and make a wish. Then they hammer a coin into the bark of the tree to keep the wish in."

"I see…" mused Ciminin.

"As your servant," continued John Smalls, "I sit by the tree, hidden from sight, and overhear all the people's troubles. If someone is truly in need, and not just wishing for riches or good luck, I come and tell you what I've heard. Then, at your command, I do what I can to help the people. But this must all remain a secret. Your people are very superstitious, and if they find out what you are doing, they will no longer trust you."

"I understand," said the queen.

"I will visit often or rarely, whatever suits you," said the little man. "To summon me, lure the jackdaw that nests by the library window with a piece of cheese. When he comes to you, tie a small string to his leg and shoo him off the ledge. He will find me."

After overhearing this, Princess Jamsine stormed away down the hall. She was furious to discover there was one more way people would love and admire her sister when they should be loving and admiring her. She spent a sleepless night staring at the velvet canopy over her bed, pounding her quail-down quilt with her fists until it spewed feathers.

Early the next morning she sat up and said, "I have to see this tree for myself." After a long, leisurely breakfast, she ordered that a coach be made ready for her, and off she went to see the wishing oak.

It took some time to find it. The woods where the oak grew were half a day's journey away and the road through them became darker and narrower the deeper they went. At last they arrived, but the appearance of the tree was not what she expected. The trunk had been broken in a storm many years before but continued to grow. It lay sideways along the bank of a rocky brook, its branches brushing the water. Coins of every sort—gold, silver and even copper pennies—were hammered deep into the rough bark. Over the years, the bark in turn had grown protectively over the coins. There were so many coins in the tree that when the sun peeked through the canopy, the trunk glinted like the scales of some monstrous dragon.

As she stood there, listening to the brook tumble over the rocks, she wondered where John Smalls hid himself to listen to the people who came here with their hopes and their coins. "They're all idiots," she muttered to herself, afraid that her guards and coachman up the hill would overhear her. "Every one of them, with their foolish wishes. Why do they all get what they want and I don't? Why can't I be queen?"

Hating the sight of all those coins, she realized that what she needed was not some silly wish, but a plan. And with a flash like lightning in her mind's eye, she knew all at once how to get what she wanted.

Full of resolve, she left the tree and climbed the bank, back up to her coach. "You there," she said to her guards, "do any of you have a coin?"

One of them fished a gold coin from his bag and gave it to her. She took it back down to the oak and found a rock to pound it into the bark. Though she said not a word out loud, she vowed to knock Ciminin off her father's throne and be sitting there herself before the week was out.

Princess Jamsine returned to the castle very late that night, but as soon as she was inside she called her personal guards and said, "Go and grab Queen Ciminin from her bed, put her in an onion bag and take her to the far, far mountains."

Her guards were surprised by this order. "But she's the queen," said one.

"And it will take many months to get there," said another.

Jamsine gave them each a bag of gold. "Perhaps this will quiet your concerns," she said. "Do it now and get out!"

The guards were happy to have the gold and so they went to Queen Ciminin's room, put her in an onion bag and took her off to the far, far mountains.

The next morning, when Queen Ciminin did not appear at the royal breakfast table, everyone began asking questions. And when she did not appear at any of her appointments that morning, the servants began to search for her. But Princess Jamsine told them to stop the search, as she knew where the queen was. She told them to expect an official announcement that afternoon.

News spread quickly about the missing queen and by

noon, a large crowd had gathered in the courtyard of the castle, waiting to hear what Princess Jamsine had to say. Everyone knew how shocked and disappointed Jamsine must have felt, being passed over for the queenship. And now they were afraid something awful had befallen Ciminin. Many people expected that Jamsine was going to lie about it. But she did not lie very much at all.

Jamsine came out onto the balcony wearing a black dress, holding one hand to her heart. "My people," she said, pausing to wipe a tear from her eye, "I have done a terrible thing. I visited the wishing oak in the north wood yesterday and I couldn't help but speak my mind. I made a wish, hoping that my sister would die so that I could be Queen of All the Land." Everyone in the courtyard gasped. "Sadly, when I returned to the castle, I found that my dear sister had tumbled down the stairs and broken her head, and I immediately knew that I had been the cause. Please, my people, I hope that you will forgive me. I promise I will make it up to you any way I can." And with that, she went back inside and pretended to cry some more.

The crowd outside erupted into riot and began throwing turnips and chair legs at the castle. But there was nothing to be done, for their beloved new queen was dead. The next day, a grand funeral was held for Queen Ciminin. Her sister put a scarecrow inside the coffin and kept it sealed so no one could see inside. The day after that, the princess was crowned Queen Jamsine of All the Land.

As for Ciminin, well, she was not at all happy about being grabbed in the middle of the night and put in an onion bag. She was even less happy about being dropped on the back of a donkey cart and taken away to the far, far mountains. As the guard had said, it took many months of travel and Ciminin was bumped and jostled the entire way. She was never once let out of the cramped bag, even to stretch her legs. The guards pushed bits of cold burnt toast and hard butter through a hole in the bag for her to eat. When they arrived, deep in the mountains and high up past the trees, she was dumped out in the snow, still in her nightgown, which was now filthy and not much more than a silken rag.

With the wind whistling around her and her bare feet freezing in the snow, her first thought was to find shelter. Perhaps there was a shepherd's hut nearby? Or a wolves' den where she could get out of the bitter wind? She walked till she couldn't feel her feet and her hands could barely hold her nightgown around her. At last she came to a huntsman's shelter. It was made of sturdy timbers and the snow was heaped on the low roof like whipped cream. Inside she found the pelts of all the creatures the huntsman had shot or trapped. The furs were piled like cords of wood and she broke one of the bales, snuggled down into the warm furs and fell fast asleep.

The next morning, she was rudely awakened by the huntsman, who was not happy at seeing his furs spread out over the dirt floor. Nevertheless, he took pity on her and said that if she worked for him, he would allow her to stay in the shelter till spring. He gave Ciminin the job of scraping the meat from the pelts, telling her that whatever she scraped, she was free to eat. And so she lived there, barely warm and barely fed, till the spring.

When Ciminin finally left the huntsman's shelter, she thanked him warmly for letting her stay there. He gave her the hide of a hare, which he had been using for years as a curtain. She was glad to have it to keep the rain from her shoulders as she began the long journey back to the castle, down valleys, across rivers and through dark, dismal woods. She ate shoots and berries and slept at night in the hollows of trees that squirrels had filled with pine cones.

Then one day she came across a young man lying in the road, his horse standing close by. She bent and tried to wake him, but found that he was dead. An old man came along as she knelt on the road beside the young man and said, "Oh, the poor prince, he has hit his head and died." The old man rode off on the prince's horse to find someone to tell. Ciminin stayed to keep the birds and animals away from the body.

When the old man returned with the prince's people, they thanked her and gave her a small bag with a blood red ruby inside. Thinking she might need the ruby badly one day, she kept the bag tied round her neck for many months of travel.

Throughout the summer, Ciminin had no trouble finding food or safe places to sleep. But when winter came again her meals grew farther and farther apart. Two hungry-looking dogs began following her and she had to carry rocks to throw at them to keep them away. Finally, after weeks of near starvation, her body shivering day and night, and still far from home, she wondered if it was now time to sell her ruby. No, she decided; things might still get worse for her, so she held off.

One day, while the snow and wind were blowing sideways, she found a cave that a farmer was using as a granary. There, for the second winter, she snuggling into the grain to keep herself warm, and lived off the rats and sparrows that crept in to steal the barley.

When spring came, she took to the road again, eating whatever she could find on the way—berries, buds, and occasionally, when she came upon a flock of magpies nattering over something dead, a few bits of rotting fish or furry creature. Once she ate something that cramped her stomach terribly. It made her feverish and dizzy and she tripped on the high road and twisted an ankle. Still, in her delirium, she kept going, thinking she had to get home before she died.

She was followed by some girls going to market who thought, seeing her ragged nightgown and the hide of a hare over her shoulders, and how she limped and staggered, that she was a lunatic or a beggar. They taunted her, not knowing she was very ill.

"Is my sister there?" Ciminin asked, all muddled in the head. "I'm trying to get home."

"You have a home?" mocked one of the girls. "What is it? A hole in the ground?"

Ciminin tried to make them understand. "No, no, it's a castle. My father was king and I'm—"

"Ha! She thinks she's a princess!" another girl crowed, laughing. "You look like an idiot beggar." And they circled around her, pushing her from one to the other, calling her names. "Ugly, stupid, princess beggar."

One of them tore the hare's hide from her shoulders and threw it into the bushes. Another grabbed the bag around her neck and pulled until the string broke, spilling the ruby onto the ground. "Well, look what we found!" the girl said. "It's a ruby!"

"My ruby...can't have my ruby," said Ciminin, thinking, in her terrible state, that she would have to sell it soon.

"Let's flip a coin," one of the girls said. "If the princess wins, she can keep the ruby. If not, she has to marry a frog."

All the girls laughed and kept pushing her. "Well? Well? What will you do?"

"My ruby," said Ciminin tearfully, thinking she might die without it. "I agree."

One of the girls raced down to a creek that ran near the road. She found a plump frog on the bank and brought it back. "Flip the coin. I have her husband here."

Another girl flipped the coin and it landed in the dirt. "You lose!" she shouted. "The ruby is mine and you have to marry this frog. Now keep him close, or you'll never get home."

They pushed her to the ground, dropped the frog on top of her and ran away with the ruby.

Ciminin held the frog to her breast, thinking, in her fevered state, that she had to protect this poor creature she had to marry. She dragged herself to the side of the road and lay there, half-crazed, half-starved, talking to herself as if she really were mad.

She was found by a washerwoman who had been working down at the creek. The washerwoman had heard the girls up on the road and climbed the bank to see what was going on. When she found Ciminin clutching the frog and babbling, she felt the girl's forehead and knew immediately she was very unwell. She ran for her husband and when the husband saw the girl, all muddled and babbling, he said, "Oh no, she's enchanted!"

"She is not," said the washerwoman. "She's ill."

"But she's got a frog and she's talking about marrying it. Either the frog is enchanted or she is."

"She's in a fever, you old fool. Now shut up and help me."

They tried to take the frog away, but Ciminin screamed and held it close. There was nothing to do but pick her up and carry her to their little house and try to nurse her back to health.

Back at the castle, people continued to grumble over the death of Queen Ciminin. Had Jamsine killed her sister, perhaps buried her alive? When all the grumbling eventually reached the queen's ear, she dealt with it swiftly. The first law she made as queen said that anyone who even mentioned her sister would be thrown into the deepest dungeon. And that was that. No one dared talk about Ciminin again.

That didn't stop Queen Jamsine from spending far too much time worrying about what she had done. Over the next several months, Jamsine came to realize how much she had relied on her sister. No matter how many new dresses she had made, she never knew if she was in fashion. She tried to speak clearly and use big words, but no one ever said she was smart. In fact, she was quite sure her ministers were talking behind her back, saying she didn't know what the big words meant. *Oh, what have I done,* she thought. *Instead of sending*

Ciminin to the far, far mountains, I should have locked her in a high tower, so I could visit and watch her and know what to do.

Still, she tried hard to be happy. She made sure she had the best of everything. Only the nicest looking wood was allowed to burn in her fireplaces. And only the best apples and grouse knuckles made it past her kitchen door. Once a month she held a fancy dress ball, hoping to meet a handsome prince. But since she only liked to talk about jewelry and shoes and clothes, all the princes thought she was terribly boring. And soon they were making excuses and turning down her invitations.

Shortly after she was crowned queen, John Smalls came to offer his services. He gave the same speech about helping people who came to tell their troubles to the wishing oak.

"I don't care about any of that," said Jamsine. "People can look out for themselves."

The little man bowed. "As you wish," he said. Then he reminded her about the large bag of gold the king had left him.

"You are here at a bad time," she told him. "My fancy dress balls are costing a fortune. I'm reduced to using ugly firewood in the castle's fireplaces, as all the pretty-looking stuff has been used up. Come back in the winter."

But when winter arrived and John Smalls appeared a second time, he was again sent away empty-handed. She had to raise the taxes, she said, and when that money came in, perhaps she could pay him then. But she never did.

Come the second spring, while Ciminin lay feverish at the washerwoman's, Queen Jamsine contracted a bit of a cough. She didn't seem terribly worried about it, but her servants became quite concerned. They tried various medicines and potions, slipping them into her tea when she wasn't looking. But nothing seemed to work. Finally, they sent for a famous doctor to help her. He had been to the castle many times before, but as he lived a long distance away, he did not visit often.

On his way to see the queen, the doctor thought he would drop his laundry off at the washerwoman's. But what did he find when he poked his head in her little door?

"I believe I know this girl!" he declared, after one glance at the girl asleep in the corner. "I thought she was dead. What on earth is she doing here?"

"Two days ago," said the washerwoman, "we found her beside the road, all crazed and feverish."

"And she has an enchanted frog!" her husband spouted.

"Hish!" said the woman, casting an angry eye his way.

"Has she spoken at all?" asked the doctor.

"Well," said the washerwoman, "every day she wakes for a little while. She says a few words, then falls back to sleep. She says she found a prince who had been thrown from his horse."

"Tell him about the furs," said her husband.

"She spoke of sleeping on furs in a huntsman's hut," the wife continued. "More furs than anyone has ever seen. And she might have been rich, as she spoke of a bag of rubies she got from the prince's people."

"And that frog!" The husband pointed. "I'm sure it's the prince himself."

"Oh, pssh!" said the washerwoman. "In her fever-talk, she thinks she has to marry this frog here. Says she won't be able to get home without him."

"Oh, the poor girl," said the doctor. "A fever can play tricks with you, that's for sure." He was in a hurry to get to the castle to treat the queen's cough. So he said he would return in a week and gave the washerwoman some money to make sure Ciminin had everything she needed to get better. "And get rid of that frog," added the doctor. "The poor thing needs to eat and be outside."

On his way to the castle, the doctor wondered what he should do. He knew that Queen Jamsine had said she accidently killed her sister and now wanted no one to remind her of it. He certainly didn't want to be thrown into the deepest dungeon for bringing up the subject. But on the other hand, wouldn't Jamsine be glad to know she hadn't killed her sister after all? Perhaps he would receive a huge reward! As he travelled along, mile after mile, he slowly convinced himself he could avoid the dungeon and end up with his pockets full of gold.

When the doctor arrived at the castle, the queen was sitting on her throne nibbling from a bowl of hummingbird elbows in apple jelly. She was the queen, after all, and could do whatever she wanted. And today she wanted hummingbird elbows.

"I heard you have a little cough, Your Majesty," said the doctor. "One has to be careful. Sometimes a cough can develop into—"

"Ahem," said the queen. "Ahem. I do not have a cough at all. I am merely having a practice at interrupting the lords and ladies who attend my monthly ball. Ahem," she said louder. "Important people always interrupt."

"I am glad you are well, Your Majesty," said the doctor. "Before I go, I have some news that may make you feel even better."

"And what is that?" asked the queen.

"I found a…relative of yours as I was travelling on the high road."

"A relative of mine?" repeated the queen. "Was it an uncle or an aunt?"

"No."

"A cousin? A grandfather? A nephew?"

"No."

The queen thought about this for a moment. Then she turned deathly pale. "Was it my…?"

The doctor could see by her pale complexion that she meant her sister Ciminin. "Yes, Your Majesty, it is true. She is quite alive."

"Guards!" the queen shouted. "Take this man and throw him into the deepest dungeon!"

The royal guards rushed into the throne room, grabbed the doctor, and threw him into the deepest dungeon. Queen Jamsine did not want anyone else to know that her sister was alive, so no one was allowed to visit the doctor.

The next day, Queen Jamsine was burning up with curiosity. She had spent the entire night lying awake, wondering how Ciminin had been living. Was she rich? Had she married well? Did people still admire how she dressed? Before breakfast, Jamsine rushed down to the deepest dungeon to speak to the doctor. "Tell me something about her," she demanded.

The doctor was not at all happy about being in the dungeon, and he was even less happy with the queen who put him there."She is alive," he said, arms crossed.

"Something more," the queen barked.

The doctor was not about to lie, but he was not going to give her more information than he had to. "Furs," he said, and paused to check the state of his fingernails.

"What?"

"She has slept on more furs than anyone has ever seen."

"And do people like her?"

The doctor thought of the washerwoman. "As far as I know," he said, "people like her just fine."

The queen turned purple. Unable to control her temper, she spun around and rushed back up the stairs. *Furs must be in fashion,* she thought. She spent the entire morning fuming over her sister. How could she be so rich? Where did she get the money to buy more furs than anyone had ever seen? Surely, that was why people liked her so much.

She called all her ministers together and said, "I need furs. We must raise the taxes so I can have the most furs."

"But Your Majesty," the ministers told her, "the people do not have any more money. You have taxed them and taxed them and now they are all poor."

The queen gave a peevish snort and sent her ministers away. *There must be money in the kingdom somewhere,* she thought. The next moment she remembered something important and called for one of her servants.

"Go to the kitchen and bring me a piece of cheese and a bit of string."

When they were brought, the queen went to the library and lured the jackdaw to the window ledge. As the jackdaw ate the cheese, she tied the string to his leg and pushed him off the ledge. The bird flew away over the town and out of sight.

Later that afternoon, John Smalls appeared in the library; from where, she couldn't tell.

"I have a job for you," said the queen. "I need money to buy furs and you know where to get it. You once told me about an oak tree in the north woods full of coins. Go there and pry out three bags of coins and bring them to me."

"But Your Majesty," said John Smalls, "these are people's wishes. No good will come of this."

"Bring me three bags of coins or I will have your head chopped off and thrown into the deepest dungeon!"

So John Smalls had to do as she demanded. He went to the north woods that day and began prying out coins. He was already angry with the queen. First, for not giving him the bag of gold the old king had left him. And second, for not letting him do his job of helping her subjects. Now she was making him undo the wishes of the honest people who had put the coins in there. What would people think when they saw their coins gone from the oak?

It was then that John Smalls had an idea. If the queen wanted the coins, she could have a few of the things the coins had sealed into the oak. If he undid the wishes, that would be some fine revenge. John Smalls didn't know the wish of every coin that he pried out of the oak, but he remembered a few. And those few would be enough.

John Smalls returned to the castle and was very busy deep in the night, particularly at the end of the castle where the queen slept. The next morning he delivered the three bags of coins to the queen in the royal library.

"How are you this morning, my queen?" asked John Smalls.

"Not so well," the queen answered. "This morning I awoke with half my hair gone. I look like a balding old crone! And there must have been a dog in my room, sleeping on my pillow. I could feel fleas biting me all through the night. So now I'm covered in red spots."

John Smalls shook his head as if to say, *That's very sad; I don't know how that could have happened.*

Nevertheless, Queen Jamsine took the three bags of coins from him. She sent merchants and messengers out to the four corners of the kingdom to buy all the furs they could find. When they returned, she had a giant bed and a beautiful coat made out of them. Then she went around the castle, parading her furs for all to see. Every minister, servant and maid bowed to her, as usual. But not a single one of them had anything to say about her fashionable new furs. What was worse, she thought she caught them pointing and whispering among themselves behind her back. Frustrated, Jamsine spun around and returned to her room.

Later that day, Jamsine could not stop thinking about her sister, especially when she was trying to decide what to wear. Every shoe, every sash, and the cut of every hem made her wonder if her sister had nicer, more fashionable things. Finally, she could stand it no more and went down to the deepest dungeon to speak to the doctor.

"Is there anything else about her that you know? Tell me now."

The doctor was in the midst of the one meal they gave him each day, a small pile of peacock bones. He stood when the queen entered the dungeon and took his time licking the grease from his fingers. "Rubies," he said.

"What?" shouted the queen. "What about rubies?"

"She had a bag of rubies."

"But do they make her popular? Do people like her more?"

"As far as I know," answered the doctor, "people like her quite well."

The queen turned purple with rage and rushed back up the dungeon stairs. Apparently rubies were in fashion and no one had told her. She spent the entire day fuming over her sister. How could she afford a whole bag of rubies? *Why don't I have a bag of rubies so people like me more?*

"You there," she said to one of her servants. "Go to the kitchen and bring me a piece of cheese and a bit of string."

When the cheese and the string were brought, the queen went to the library and lured the jackdaw to the window ledge. As the jackdaw ate the cheese, she tied the string to his leg and pushed him off the ledge. The bird flew away over the town and out of sight.

A short while later, John Smalls appeared in the library; from where, she couldn't tell.

"I have another job for you," said the queen. "I need money to buy rubies and you know where to get it. Go to the oak in the north woods and pry out five bags of coins and bring them to me."

"But Your Majesty—"

"Hush!" shouted the queen. "Bring me five bags of coins or I will have your head chopped off and thrown into the deepest dungeon!"

John Smalls had to do as she demanded. He went to the north woods that day and began prying out coins. This time, he remembered more of the people's wishes and made a note of them. Then he returned to the castle and he was again very busy deep into the night. The next morning he delivered the five bags of coins to the queen in the royal library.

"How are you this morning, my queen?" asked John Smalls.

"Not so well," the queen answered. "I must have had some spoiled meat, for I have been running to the royal bathroom every two minutes. I had the spots, and that was bad enough. But now I have the trots. And look at my hair!"

John Smalls shook his head as if to say, *That's very sad; I don't know how that could have happened.*

Nevertheless, Queen Jamsine took the five bags of coins. She sent merchants and messengers out to buy all the rubies they could find and had them made into a beautiful necklace. Then she paraded around the castle to show off her new ruby necklace to everyone. But her ministers and servants had not been paid in several months, and she could tell by their looks they were not impressed by her necklace, no matter how fashionable it was.

All that afternoon, Jamsine could not keep thoughts of her sister from her mind. Was she married? Was she happy? Was someone buying her all these beautiful things? So down she went to the deepest dungeon to speak to the doctor.

"Is there anything else about her that you know? Tell me, or I will have your head chopped off and thrown . . . over there."

The doctor stood and clasped his hands gently before him. "She met a handsome prince," he said.

"What?" said the queen, feeling the blood rise to her head. "Where?"

"On the road. I believe that's how she got the bag of rubies."

"So he's handsome and rich," the queen said to herself. "What else, man?"

"It wasn't really clear," the doctor mused. "She was very feverish. Something about an enchanted frog she's going to marry."

"What? What?" shouted the queen, completely confused. "She's getting married to him? To it?"

The doctor nodded. "Apparently. But as I say, she was quite unwell at the time and had to let the frog go."

The queen let out a little squeak of a cry and rushed back up the dungeon stairs, purple with rage. She spent the entire day (on the royal toilet) fuming over her sister. *So,* she thought, *the prince has been enchanted and turned into a frog. My sister was feverish and let the frog go. Ha! Now that's how to get a prince to marry me. All I have to do is find him before my sister does!*

"You there, guard!" she shouted through her door. "Go to the kitchen and bring me some cheese and string."

When they were brought, the queen went to the library and lured the jackdaw to the window ledge. As the jackdaw ate the cheese, she tied the string to his leg and pushed him off the ledge. The bird flew away over the town and out of sight.

A short while later, John Smalls appeared in the library; from where, she couldn't tell.

"I have one more job for you," said the queen. "I need money to find all the frogs in the kingdom. One of them is a prince and I'm going to marry him. Go to the oak in the north woods and pry out seven bags of coins and bring them to me."

John Smalls opened his mouth to speak, but the queen silenced him. "Just bring me the seven bags of coins. Or else!" she added irritably.

And John Smalls had to do as she ordered. He went to the north woods that day and began prying out coins. And this time around, he remembered even more of the people's wishes and made a note of them. He did not have the luxury of choosing this coin over that. To make up seven bags, he had to dig out nearly every coin he could find.

He returned to the castle and again was busy deep into the night. The next morning he delivered the seven bags of coins to the queen in the royal library.

"How are you this morning, my queen?" asked John Smalls.

"Not so well," said the queen. "It felt as though there were rocks in my bed all night, so I've woken all sore and twisted. I had the spots and the trots, and that was bad enough. But now I have an aching back. And look at my hair!"

John Smalls shook his head as if to say, *That's very sad; I don't know how that could have happened.*

Nevertheless, Queen Jamsine took the seven bags of coins. This time, she used the coins to hire men and women all over he kingdom to bring her every frog they could find. For surely, one of them was the prince that Ciminin had foolishly let go in her fever.

Hour after hour, the people arrived at the castle with boxes and baskets of frogs. Each frog was worth a penny and every bushel of frogs was worth a gold coin. Jamsine set herself up in the throne room to kiss each frog and wait to see if it turned into a prince. By noon she had kissed six hundred frogs and her lips were getting red from all the kissing. By the middle of the afternoon she had kissed twelve hundred of them and still there was a line of people waiting with baskets of frogs. The line stretched outside the castle and down the main street of the town for half a mile.

Once the frogs had been kissed, the servants opened the kitchen door at the back of the castle and let them go. But of course, it was only a matter of time before people started gathering them up and bringing them around to the front to be kissed again.

By the third day, the queen was getting frustrated at not finding her prince. Her lips were tired from frog-kissing. And her mouth had broken out in big red and white bumps that made it painful to eat or drink.

That afternoon, a small boy brought the queen a frog in a little wooden box. The queen's servant paid the boy a penny for his frog and shooed him away. But as the boy got back outside he stopped and looked carefully at the coin in his hand. All the people still in line with their frogs pointed and smiled at how cute the boy was.

Then the boy said in a puzzled way, "Hey, this is my penny."

A woman standing next to him said, "Well, of course it is. You earned it from our crazy queen."

"No, no," said the boy. "This is the penny I put into the wishing oak when my mother was sick."

The woman came up close to look at the coin. "How would you know? All pennies look alike."

"No, they don't," the boy said. "I put an X on my penny when my grandmother gave it to me. I put the X over the queen's eye and made a wish with it. And here it is! Someone must have taken it out of the oak tree. Now my wish is no good."

"There, there, my boy," said the woman next to him.

But the boy cried. "I don't want my mother to get sick again!"

By then, everyone nearby who was standing in line was looking at the coins they had gotten from the castle already.

"Here's a coin from the cobbler! He always pokes a hole in his coins so he can carry them on a string."

"That doesn't mean anything," said someone in line behind him. "It doesn't mean it came from the oak."

The people conferred and decided to send someone to check the wishing oak to see if coins were missing from its bark. Two horsemen volunteered, as no one else wanted to lose their place in line, and off they went to check the tree.

Meanwhile, at the washerwoman's, Ciminin had mostly recovered. She was still a bit weak, but very glad to be warm and fed under the washerwoman's roof. She had heard about the doctor's visit, how he had left money for food and clothing. She also heard all about the frog she had thought, in her fever, she had to marry.

"How silly," she said. "Who would ever think of marrying a frog?"

After a few more days, well-rested, well-fed and wearing a new dress that the washerwoman had bought for her, she took her leave of the washerwoman and her husband and made her way to the castle through the northern forest.

Now, when the two horsemen arrived at the wishing oak, they found the ancient tree stripped of almost all of the coins that had been pounded into it over the years. A terrible sense of doom came over them, as they thought that all the good the tree had done had now been undone.

"But who would do this?" asked the first horseman.

"That's easy," said the other. "Just follow the bad luck."

"You mean the queen?"

"Everyone knows about her spots and her trots and her aching back. She has all the things people have wished to be rid of. And have you seen her hair?"

The horsemen were about to return to the castle to tell people the news when they saw Ciminin coming down the high road. Their eyes grew to the size of saucers. "How can this be?" asked the one.

The other slapped his knee and said joyfully, "I understand! They took Jamsine's wish out, too. She wished that her sister would die so she could be queen. It came true. Now her coin is out and her wish is undone!" And the two rushed up to Ciminin and bowed before her, calling her their true queen.

After all she had endured, Ciminin was glad to be recognised as herself and not some thief or beggar. One of the men gave her his horse to ride and as they returned to the castle, they caught Ciminin up on all the news—the poverty of the kingdom and the theft of the coins from the oak for Jamsine's furs and rubies and frogs. And of course she heard all about her sister's terrible ailments.

One of the horsemen rode on ahead to announce that Ciminin had come back to life because the coin had been taken from the wishing oak. By the time she neared the castle, half the people were dancing and singing in the streets for joy at her return. The other half were storming the castle in anger to be rid of Jamsine—especially since she had run out of coins to pay them for the frogs they'd collected.

Hearing about the return of her sister and seeing the riot outside, the queen gathered up her skirts and rushed out the kitchen door of the castle, with her spots and her trots and her aching back, never to be heard from again.

Well, that's not entirely true. Months later she was found by a farmer, drowned in the black water of a lily pond. Seeing her terrible hair, the farmer thought she was an old crone. "The poor thing," he said as he dragged her body from the water. "She must have died trying to catch frogs for that horrible queen we used have. I'm sure her last wish was that she'd stayed in bed that morning. Oh well, at least the old thing died fashionably dressed."

Ciminin was once again crowned Queen of All the Land. A huge celebration was held, using the proceeds from the sale of Jamsine's furs and rubies and other extravagances. In a special ceremony afterward, the washerwoman, who had nursed her back to health, and the doctor, who had been swiftly brought out of the dungeon, were given all the royal court's finest honours and medals.

After the dinner, when all of the guests had left, one of the castle guardsmen came up to Ciminin and said there was someone waiting to speak to her in the royal library.

"He is quite, um…an unusual gentleman," said the guard, "and he says it is very important."

Ciminin hurried to the library. "John Smalls," she said as the little man bowed before her. "I have been expecting you. Here is the bag of gold my father promised you."

"Thank you, my queen," said John Smalls.

"Are you here to help me?" asked Ciminin.

"Alas," said John Smalls, holding his hat. "I served your father well and am very thankful for his kindness. But I am now too old to help you anymore. I am hoping you will allow my son to continue my work and serve you faithfully in the coming years."

He gestured to someone in the room behind her and the queen turned. And there was a young man of about her age, more handsome than any man she had ever laid eyes on. He held his hat in his hand like his father, but unlike him, he was not knee high, but tall and strong.

"My queen," he said with a small bow.

Ciminin turned back to John Smalls with a barely concealed smile and asked, "Is he to fulfill wishes as you have done?"

"That is correct," said John Smalls.

"Then I believe he will do nicely," said Ciminin.

And so, things returned to normal in the kingdom. Tax money was spent on roads and bridges instead of ball gowns and grouse knuckles. The servants and ministers were glad to have a cheerful and learned ruler who couldn't wait to get out of bed in the morning. And as the jackdaw that nested by the library window grew fat, the people grew happy and prosperous, knowing they couldn't have wished for a better queen.

CPSIA information can be obtained at www.ICGtesting.com
Printed in the USA
LVOW10s0340041115

460985LV00001B/12/P